The Women

of

As Mulheres de Tijucopapo

Tijucopapo

Marilene Felinto

Translated and with an afterword by Irene Matthews

University of Nebraska Press, Lincoln and London

Originally published in
Portuguese as *As Mulheres
de Tijucopapo*, copyright
© 1982 by Marilene Felinto
Copyright © 1994 by the
University of Nebraska
Press. All rights reserved
Manufactured in the
United States of America
The paper in this book
meets the minimum
requirements of American
National Standard for
Information Sciences –
Permanence of Paper for
Printed Library Materials,
ANSI Z39.48-1984. Library
of Congress Cataloging-in-
Publication Data
Felinto, Marilene, 1957-
[Mulheres de Tijucopapo.
English] The women of
Tijucopapo=As mulheres
de Tijucopapo / by Marilene
Felinto; translated and with
an afterword by Irene
Matthews. p. cm. –
(Latin American women
writers) Includes biblio-
graphical references.
ISBN 0-8032-1988-1 (alk. paper).
ISBN 0-8032-6881-5 (pbk.)
I. Title.   II. Series.
PQ9698.16.E446M813   1994
869.3 – dc20 93-43538 CIP

Contents

Note on the Translation

As I was working on the English translation of *As Mulheres de Tijucopapo*, a second edition of the novel was published by Editora 34 in Brazil. The appearance of a second edition confirms a continuing appreciation for Marilene Felinto's first novel, while the eleven-year delay between the two editions confirms – perhaps – the relative difficulty of both the theme and the language of the novel.

My first drafts in English were too stilted and also too gentle for the harsh message and tone of the original Portuguese. I had to take care to maintain both the short, sharp sentences of Marilene Felinto's writing and the novel's elliptical structure: Key phrases reappear at different moments, sometimes identical and sometimes slightly, subtly, changed to move the theme or the understanding of the characters onward. I have also tried to retain the verb play used in the original. Brazilian Portuguese moves easily in and out of tenses, present, past, and future; such a game reads more unusually in English, but I have kept to the original tenses to give a similar impression of moving through reality into memory and on to aspiration, and back again, albeit arbitrarily. Finally, Marilene Felinto uses a colloquial, personal, sometimes childlike language for much of the dialogue in the novel, including the dialogue the narrator, Risia, sustains with herself and her memories. I hope I have been able to convey some of the facile and the familiar in such language, but I hope also that I have not anglicized it to the point of losing the obsessively immature and reiterative nature of the search into and out of the truth of the self. When there was a choice to be made between rendering the original in a literal but perhaps "awkward" English, or finding an equivalent English phrase that was less noticeable but also less accurate, I generally opted for the former, since Marilene Felinto's own semantics and syntax are not intended to be smooth or artless, but spirited and discontinuous.

This translation would have been impossible without the collaboration of Marilene Felinto herself, who read an early draft, corrected many vernacular incomprehensions on my part, and pushed me to render her text in hard, unforgiving prose. I had visited Pernambuco and Recife, but I needed Marilene to describe to me some of the many fruits and games and places of the Northeast referred to in the novel. As far as possible, I sought an English equivalent for their names, even if there were no direct synonyms; in a few cases, I resorted to leaving the original term and explaining it in the brief glossary at the end of the text. There, the reader will find *Lampião* and *macaco* and *Higienópolis*, along with some of the tropical fruits and birds so important to Risia's nostalgic recollections of the region of her childhood.

I was able to meet Marilene Felinto personally and get her reactions to the English text during a five-week visit to Brazil in the summer of 1992, with funding from the National Endow-

viii

ment for the Humanities and the support and the company of a group led by Saúl Sosnowski and Phyllis Butler, of the Department of Spanish and Portuguese at the University of Maryland, College Park. This was a wonderfully productive and intensive seminar (with just a wee bit of time for shopping). Organized Research support from Northern Arizona University allowed me the time to finish my draft.

On the work of translation, in addition to the comments of Marilene Felinto and her friends I had very helpful advice from one anonymous reader and, especially, from Naomi Lindstrom, herself a dauntingly expert but unfailingly generous translator of Brazilian and Hispanic American literature. I spent a couple of short but useful and entertaining sessions of cultural critique with Claudia Reis, a Carioca who knows her Northeastern stuff too.

Finally, I should particularly like to thank Francine Masiello for her tremendous encouragement and for her intellectual friendship before, during, and after this particular project. It seems to have taken a whole gang of us to get Marilene Felinto's highly individual words to you, the reader – we hope you enjoy them!

Irene Matthews

The Women *of* Tijucopapo

I celebrate myself and sing myself.

WALT WHITMAN

*I was to blame, or rather, that harsh life
was to blame, for giving me a harsh soul.*

GRACILIANO RAMOS

If I could dedicate this story . . .

1

By the time I get there, I certainly will have seen flowers, I want to see red flowers. By the time I get there, I'll have gone by beds of flowers in the middle of the fields, and I'm going to translate this letter into English and send it.

I want what I may say to sound like English, another language I know how to speak, a foreign language. Saying "Good-bye, mother!" "Good-bye, father!" "Good-bye, everyone" sometimes strikes me as much more suitable than "Adeus mae! pai! vocês!"

I haven't seen any flowers yet. I want to see flowers. On the road there are babassu palm trees and shacks. I remembered yesterday that mama was born in Tijucopapo. If there's a war, she's to blame.

It was in Tijucopapo that my mother was born. Although all that is hidden from me. But still I do know about what she told me in moments of sad desperation, and about what I know I am, and about what comes from her, and about what I heard inside her belly, and about what is traced on her brow and in our fate, my fate and hers.

My mouth is filled with dirt, it tastes of red, I spit grit, I grind my teeth. I was five years old and I was eating dirt and shitting roundworms like crazy, my eyes bulging out like a dolphin's; that didn't stop me from stampeding out the next day, however, and sliding from the top to the bottom of the mound of dirt, wrapping myself in dirt, and rolling in it, and eating and spitting and shitting and bawling into the four winds to go tell them: "You go to hell and take my worms with you, papa and mama, and take your quarreling and your quarreling about me and your quarrels that make me cry so hard. Go with my pinworms, with my *Giardias* . . ." And I'd crumble the dirt into dust and pour it over my head. I'd emerge from there, at the end of the afternoon, grubby as a trucker's helper, satisfied, nourished, and knowing that if papa got a hold of me I'd be in for a beating.

Papa almost always caught me. I'd already had plenty of sound beatings.

The only thing I know is my mother was born in Tijucopapo. A place where the earth is black. All the rest is a mystery, not even she knows. I'm the only one who knows.

I'm going to see if the letter can be in English. It would come out easier in English; places and the names of houses and people sound more resonant in English, just like in the movies.

I'm still not too sure why I am out here, heading away. It seems I made some comparisons and they weren't any good. I want to see flowers.

2

My mother was born and I was hoping to see my salvation in that. But it isn't . . . But once I worked in a hospital and I almost vomited my innards up. I'd already vomited a few times in my life and my mother hadn't been able to stop it. I was fifteen years old and that's when I worked in a hospital and met a woman who had a lover. That woman, impressed by my intelligent conversation – and me impressed by her secret – made me her friend and confidant. She came to me to cry over the pain of having a husband you don't love, and having a pretty little daughter with that husband, and wanting a lover, wanting true love. She had tried to commit suicide twice with pills and cutting her wrists. She was thirty-three years old, beginning to get a few wrinkles, and her face wasn't all that pretty. I was crazy about her story, and also, in comparison to her, I felt wholesome, young and pure, brand-new. But one day, just once, that woman arrived at the hospital with her clothes all wrinkled, the same clothes she'd come in the day before. I'd bent down to pick something up off the floor when she comes in and goes by me: "Yesterday I slept with him," in a whisper. I raised my head slowly and looked at her face – it was a face full of guilt and stinking of semen. What kind of stench was it coming from under that woman's skirts? I declared a stink of semen mixed with brown menstrual blood which must have been that woman's. I declared what a foul stench. I declared: my father's women! My father's women! And I shot out to the bathroom and practically vomited my innards up. There must be something supersensitive in my stomach. Well, I couldn't look that woman in the face for days afterwards.

I was always very intelligent. And I hurt myself. And all I got for it was ageing spinsters ruined by their lovers or unsatisfied by their husbands who were deceiving them too.

My father's women, his mistresses, were called Analice. Later on I had a rival called Diana, and then I met a married woman who had a lover – that woman was Babiana – and then I had still another rival called Estefânia. If there's one thing I can't stand, it's betrayal.

I had to get away, and here I am, who knows how many miles out on the road that'll take me back to Tijucopapo.

I wanted to tell you about the life of Brother Jorge and Sister Naninha. Their life confirms what I want to show in a letter maybe in English. I want to show a life without betrayals. So that people won't believe it. I like to see people disbelieving what I alone believe in. It's my way of knowing that I've seen more than they have, that I know more, that I can get along on my own without them.

Sister Naninha is the only woman called Ana whose name doesn't bring betrayal to my mind. For if only I could, I'd exchange all the names of Ana for Eve, the sinner. All Anas are traitors. Let's get them the hell out. Let's run them out of paradise.

Once I was walking in the street in São Paulo and they shouted at me:

"Hey, goody-goody! Hey, Miss Morals! There goes Miss Holy-Moley herself. Old Bible-thumper."

I hit one of them on the shin with a stone:

"So's your mother!"

And I ran off crying. But I got my own back. I got my own back by bad-mouthing their mother. Your mother is something that affects you the most. I always get my own back on those morons' mother. Because they dare to insult me right on the street. And they don't even know me.

I wanted to show the lives of Sister Lourdes and Mr. Manuel

4

who lived on Abreu e Lima Street. People nowadays would be even less likely to believe they existed. Who's ever seen old guys and old gals like them? People like ... People who ... Well, when I used to go around to Abreu e Lima I was a little girl. There was a slope of hard red earth there and I'd slide down it from top to bottom like a little goat and I'd go back home covered in red and with my clothes all torn and, if papa saw me, I'd get a beating. I had a mania for sliding down dirt slopes and piles of sand. I had a mania for getting beatings.

Nowadays, I have to behave myself. Imagine that: I'm well-behaved now.

That letter I'm going to send, I wanted it to be in a foreign language, so that people wouldn't quite understand it. That way the facts would be more international, don't you think? A war code.

They told me I live as if I was at war. On the warpath. And I definitely do, and I'd add that I live in combat, under bomb attack, in conflict. And I won't calm down till I kill someone. When I was a little girl, I always clung on to the idea that I would kill my father. I didn't kill him. I wouldn't kill him now. But the desire to kill someone still remained.

Maybe I'm traveling to get married. Because that power I have of killing someone terrifies me. Only a husband, a child, and a little white house could, if not extinguish, at least control that force in me. And (I'm going to whisper this) that's the very same force that makes me capable of being a prostitute, a homosexual, a madwoman, a drunkard, an outlaw, an outsider. And, no, I'm not the type to put up with living on the outside edges of life. On the edges, I'm a thread that will break. On the edges, only strong people remain. I'm weak, delicate, fragile. But, if I were a man, or if women were allowed to, I'd go off to war. I'll volunteer for every war until they kill that force in me for anything else besides being a married woman in a little white house.

Once I saw my father call my mother "fish-face!"

I crumbled dirt into dust and poured it over my head as if I was a queen flinging on her crown, or as if I was a bride flinging on her veil.

I'm going to have to see why my mother was born there, in Tijucopapo. And, if there should be a war, she's to blame.

I know I'm going to stop many times before I carry on. For the facts aren't just one fact. Tijucopapo runs into the street I lived on up there in Recife.

3

The street where I lived was a street of Protestants, from one end to the other. The people called each other "Brother," but each house had its yard. And you don't get anywhere trying to hide the yard of a house because when I was just a little girl, I used to find them out and watch them. For each brother at the door of the church there was a brother at the door of the yard. I could scarcely stop myself from laughing. Because – get a load of this – I remember that in Lita's house there was a guava tree. And guava is the same color as a bite. As exposed gums. As the roof of your mouth. My first taste of guava was at Lita's house. There was a big yard at the back. It was there one day that I saw Lita, Carmelita – get this! – (her name was Carmelita), sort of copulating with Santo. Bearing in mind that the door of the church is closed against copulation, and bearing in mind that, in the case of Lita, Carmelita, copulation only takes place behind a dozen locks and bolts. And bearing in mind that Carmelita always revealed herself to be quite different in the yard of the red guava tree, so different that she'd pretty well got me convinced, me as I played around there in those backyards, that women are on the crazy side and men are just a bit less. My street had women in it who carried their Bible under their arm and wore long skirts at the door of the church, and, at the door that gave on to the guava tree, went in for copulation after a beating. The men on my street, those brothers, always used to beat up on their wives. And Santo used to beat up on Lita because I'd heard that too. Copulating in the doorway was the only way they had of forgiving each other.

So much for that, but before that my mother had been born. And it had happened in Tijucopapo. It was 1935 and I can't imagine how things might have been, how one could have been, how one could be born. How could one have been in 1935? Me believe in a time that comes before me? But for sure, my mother does exist. It was 1935; all the rays of the moon stole from the black sky lighting the way along a path through the hills along which the donkey walked bouncing its panniers. My grandmother wasn't even whipping the beast; she arrived sluggishly, her hair knotted against the nape of her neck. My grandmother was so black that she crawled. She was bringing my mother, who was to be given away. My mother came in a donkey pack. My mother was given away on a moonlit night. My grandmother couldn't manage any longer. This was her tenth child, at least. She couldn't kill another child from that sort of starvation made up of flour and dry salt beef and constant drought. My mother would be given away. My mother was very fresh, like a nestling. I cried like never before.

I cried like never before.

I cried like never before many times.

One day I lost the love of a man and I walked five hundred thousand miles crying from death and fear. Crying like never before. Crying so hard you wouldn't believe it.

I'm heading towards Tijucopapo now; after papa, mama – and

the loss of love. And I still don't know if I blame mankind, or the city, for that. The city is São Paulo. Will there be a war?

I'm going back to Tijucopapo, I'll go by where I was in 1964.

I cried like never before in 1964. It was Christmas.

It was Christmas in 1964. Ismael would be mama's sixth child. Mama had gone out to the center of Recife with the lamps burned out on our Christmas tree. The Christmas tree was mama's attempt to give us a Christmas. Since papa had other women and couldn't care less about us. Papa had other women. Papa couldn't care less about us.

It was late afternoon, mama went out with the lamps. The walls of the houses smelled of new paint. From here on the street I could see the table laid in Juliet's house, the house with the television set. It was the only house in the street with television and plenty of good food. But at midnight we'd all get together and for me there'd be, maybe, a piece of turkey and a whole Guaraná.

A whole bottle of soda. A premonition of war.

It was 1964 and in that year, some day or another, I can never forget that I was downtown with Ruth, drinking a whole Guaraná – the first time I'd ever drunk a whole Guaraná; Ruth had bought it, so there we were on that boiling hot day in March, one ice-cold Guaraná for me, another one for her, when suddenly, right in the middle of us, the Revolution burst out. I left my Guaraná behind on the middle of the bar counter, Ruth hauling me terrified by the hand, shops closing up, soldiers on every side, and dogs, and sirens, and bombs. And there were no more buses, and Ruth was almost crying out loud in desperation that we had to get away, no matter how, because it was really dangerous. "But what happened?" I asked. "The Revolution, the Revolution, child." And then I saw we were jammed inside a crowded green bus that wasn't ours. Where could we be going? That wasn't our bus. Revolution – my Guaraná on top of the counter, my house with no television.

At Christmas 1964 what happened was that mama weighed a lot and weighed me right down. Mama pregnant was my torment, my cross, my nine months. For every month that that belly stretched further outwards, that bitter face – mama's – shrank inwards. I started walking behind her like someone who's afraid that a deadweight will drop at any moment – I was ready to gather up the weight in my own hands. I got to walking like a crazy cockroach, I hardly ever played, I hardly ever slept, hardly ever ate. "What's wrong, mama?" I would weepily try to hint. But I'd stop myself first, I didn't dare. So I was left with the anguish of wanting to know: "What was it you swallowed that makes you look like that with that belly and that face? Is it nasty? Is it bitter? Oh, mama."

Then papa would arrive and I'd put on my assassin's face to kill him. And I'd shoot him through with a glance as if to cry out, sword at the ready:

"Papa! What did you do to mama so she's got that belly and that shitty face?"

Papa, you son of a bitch. Mama, your shitty face.

It was only later that I discovered my grandmother had been a real whore, and that my father had absorbed, therefore, that hatred of his that turned him into a man who was a not-father, a not-husband. Papa was a man without love. Could that be it? That was how I'd justify it later on. And so I exempted him from all blame. The blame comes from below those cities sedimented into the rocks that winds blew on for thousands and thousands of years. It comes from my great-grandmother and stretches to me through my papa. Either all of us are to blame, or none of us is to blame. That's why nowadays I wouldn't kill my father any

9

more. And that's why, though it was what I wanted for the longest time, I'll never ever have my name and my photo in black and white on posters in the city streets: **Wanted: for parricide.**

But as for my hating my father, yes, I really hated him. And I incorporated that hatred into everything that messes me up. Because hatred, boy, hatred is fire.

4

Mama wore a dress of red linen, a narrow tube that split open during that pregnancy. There was mama in her red dress, pummeling the clothes in the washtub, wringing them out and spreading them on the grass to bleach. Mama's pregnancy was my torture, my nine months. There would be a war. I played in the yard in the shade of mama's displeasure, of mama's tedium. But the trunk of the breadfruit tree, and the mango and the avocado, also gave shade, a different shade, which mama should have seen. Mama didn't see anything. Her belly rose up to the level of her eyes. And that belly contained everything. It contained us, the children that she had had, it held her husband, her mother, her life. Her life in her belly. Only, Ismael would be born dead. And when mama's red shadow got to be too much for me – since I was seeing everything to extremes – I'd climb up into one of those trees and spend hours in the shade of the limbs that weren't mama's. Mama was all twigs: a flowerless rosebush, dry, parched.

When midday struck, my school time, mama would start braiding my hair, sobbing with a headache. The tears rolled down her face and the braids dangled heavily down my back. Mama wept. Sometimes out loud. She said it was the headache. But as far as I was concerned, it was papa. I knew what it was. She wept into my braids and I went off to school like an execution victim dissolving into hair pomade. I've never been able to like braids since then. I've never again liked midday, my school time.

When it's midday nowadays, in São Paulo where I'm leaving from, and I walk down the street, they still shout at me that I'm Miss Goody-goody. They still try to define me, those bastards. And they don't even know me. I get back at them with stones. I'll never let anyone define me.

All I know is that it was the end of the afternoon that Christmas 1964, and the children were still playing in the street when I stopped. We were all clean, waiting for midnight. New clothes, new shoes. My dress was blue, with beads embroidered on the yoke. I was very proud of that dress. Because the beads sparkled at night and I always liked lights and shininess. But all of a sudden I stopped playing. To stop playing is to stop living. I stopped playing many times because of mama. It was mama who gave me life and death. I've died so often. She made me a dress with beads on it for Christmas and went out with the Christmas tree lights burned out and didn't come back soon. She was the light and the darkness. So didn't I stop playing and yell the place down for my mama? It was past nine o'clock and mama still hadn't come back from town. I was playing a game of kings-and-commoners when my aunt stopped me in the street and I almost fell down; people had an obsession for yanking me on the arm when I was playing to remind me that you weren't supposed to play out there and so you were supposed to stop, dead. People would come up and remind me about death: me, the one that loved life.

"Your mother hasn't come home yet and I'm worried. Come to the corner with me."

My heart thundered under the nightmare that mama might not come back:

"Is she in danger, auntie?"

Yes, it's dangerous. Mama on the street with that belly at this hour. In that state (mama was always in some sort of special state). Yes, it was dangerous. But God was great. If God willed it, anything could be done. God, please God . . . And I walked up and down the street with auntie waiting for the next bus. In the shadow of auntie's anguish. I lived a lot in the shadow of some people's anguish. Now I'm the one who's anguished and no one can stand me. I'm in a state of drunkenness and I've never touched a drop.

At ten o'clock I started thinking thoughts about mama in danger. And what if midnight came and mama hadn't come home? Sweet Jesus! Mamaaaaa . . . And I bawled the place down with the news that I wanted my mama. And I wept like never before. I sobbed convulsively. I wept so hard you wouldn't believe it.

Mama got off the bus at half past ten. I saw her blue dress strolling along. It was made of linen, too. She arrived calm and leisurely. I dried my tears shamefacedly. Because – I was sure – mama would look at me as she never had before, she would hug me as she never had before. What happened was that mama had decided to wait for an empty bus. And she'd arrived calm and dawdling. And she'd scarcely even looked at me, and she didn't hug me at all. I shamefacedly dried my tears. Mama never used to hug me.

Mama wore me out with indifference. Mama was a shit.

5

I think a lot so as to see if by comparing one thing with another I can work things out better.

But in São Paulo it was very difficult and so, among other

things, I used to lie. I got to the point of actually lying. I would lie without rhyme or reason. I lied out of pure pleasure. I would say that I'd gone to the movies yesterday even though I hadn't, if I wanted to. Among other things, too, everything frightened me more than it should have done. I wish to God I could confess my anguish. Not knowing how was an anguish. I would think about Recife.

How was it they explained, then, the ghost on my street, that street? What envelope sealed it up and turned it into an anonymous letter sent to every name and address? Was it only my house? Or was it the whole of Recife? It was the whole of Recife. It could only be the whole of Recife. I wish to God I could be supplied with statistics. If so, would I talk about the tame unsexed Protestants in the doorway of the church and the rude bestialities at the foot of the guava tree? If so, would I talk about how, on the avenue that passed by the corner of my street, the sun melted the asphalt at midday and I went to school with sunstroke? What sense did all that make in the long run? So many waves on the beach? On the asphalt? I could talk about how at the corner of my street the sun was roasting and scrambled people's brains at midday and that's how it was in Recife. Recife, the loveless. Recife, sunstruck, afire, unruly, possessed. Unloving. Diabolical Recife. Recife: soulless, diseased, virulent.

Today I wander the world with a big headache. Midday is the worst time. I've already been to one doctor after another. My headache comes from life. And it began with the birth of my mother. And now it extends to every part of me. Every part of my body that travels. That travels to see if it can be reborn in Tijucopapo where mama was born.

Yesterday I dreamed that Luciana was watching me through the opening in the shack I was sleeping in. I woke up frightened to death by that dream.

It was from Luciana on that I knew, and that Nema knew (you knew, Nema, you knew), and that my malfunction was proven, and my suffering, and my midday head for the whole of my destiny that followed . . . that followed, let's say, Luciana, a girl in the same class as me, Luciana who sent me a letter knowing very well – because I made it clear, I always made it a point to make things clear, I always took pleasure in actually disclosing certain things – that I didn't like her, that I couldn't stand her face.

I didn't like Luciana. I couldn't stand her face. But not her, she persisted. I really didn't quite know why. She would hang around at break time. She was fascinated by me. She wanted to join my group, I told her no. But she insisted. And I never knew why. Unless it was because I was a very good student, which I was, or because I drew nice posters, which always got first place, or because I was the leader of my group, or because I got a hundred in math. Unless it was for all the things I was and she wasn't. Luciana was just a docile girl who liked me. And she liked me just like that, for no reason. She liked me for myself. And she only knew how to like people and be docile. And she would come up to me like someone who likes to like and tell me:

"I like you."

And I couldn't stand her. Couldn't stand her. Just couldn't stand her.

I had doubts and I didn't believe her. Or maybe I did believe her, and that's why I couldn't stand her. I was crazy. I am crazy. But Luciana was so docile that she made you sick. I had got used to rough souls.

And it's not that I never liked anyone. That's not it. It's just that I'm the one who chooses. The one who chooses is me. I get to speak and I'm the one who chooses. When I get chosen it seems like I can't stand it.

14

But, you know, there was . . . Libânia. Whom I liked because
. . . I don't know. I liked Libânia because she was so clean and
pretty, because her notebooks were tidy and her writing so
pretty, and her hair was smooth and mine was curly, and, and . . .
Libânia had a calmness that I didn't have. It was as if I wanted to
be Libânia a little bit. I wanted to be like Libânia. Whereas Luciana repelled me with that docility of hers which I didn't want
to have because I couldn't. Libânia was an individual. Libânia
had personality. And Libânia had a father. Boy! Libânia had a father who came to fetch her from school every day in his station
wagon. And I had never been in a car, well, almost never except
when I went out with Nema and she'd take a taxi.

So I liked Libânia and I have to admit I hung around her at rec.
Not so stupidly as the way Luciana spied on me, for sure, but in a
different way. An intelligent and disguised way. I hung around
Libânia until one day we were friends and I was in her house
spending the afternoon, playing, jumping along the riverbank
teasing the fish, running around, riding in the station wagon,
and eating cookies baked in the kitchen of Libânia's spotless
house.

I was liking someone too.

The only thing that frightens me is my cruelty.

Because, first of all, I didn't reply to Luciana's letter. I ignored
it. How come she dared to send me a letter if I couldn't stand her
face? The letter was a request to be friends and to enter into my
group. Luciana was a request. And I don't like people who ask for
things. I like people who get things. That's the way I was in that
life at school.

A few days went by and Luciana told on me to Miss Penha,
our teacher. Miss Penha immediately announced out loud, looking straight at me in the class:

"All letters received should be replied to."

Miss Penha always had it in for me. It was inevitable. Damn it, Miss Penha. Damn it. And if I don't want to reply to the letter? Damn it, I thought to myself. But now that the command was to reply, I'd do it. Very well, I'll reply. And I got home and replied in five or six lines:

Luciana,
I hate you. Luciana, don't write me any more letters. Luciana, I don't like you. Stop looking at me with your dead fish-face. I can't stand your face. Don't follow me around at playtime. I don't want you in my group because you are a real dunce. You don't know how to play. You are a stupid tattletale, OK?

That was that.

At the time there was a piece of music played on the radio a lot, a sad, slow melody called "Luciana." A song to Luciana. I would never hear that music again without a confused feeling of guilt making my eyes water. Never. After Miss Penha got hold of the letter, never ever again. Since Miss Penha got hold of the letter, my heart took on a new way of beating. A stifled beat. A miserable beat. But I was such a little girl. Miss Penha always had it in for me. It was inevitable. Miss Penha sat down astonished in front of me, the letter in her hand, Luciana by her side, Luciana wiping the end of a sob from her nose with a wrinkled handkerchief. It was the most shameful day in my life. I never imagined Luciana could be such a tattletale. It never once crossed my mind that she would have the courage to defend herself. And she showed the letter to Miss Penha. To Miss Penha! That letter, a criminal act, couldn't be shown to anyone.

I was repentant and horrified by my crime.

Luciana had been my first opportunity to not like. And I took advantage of that. Boy, did I take advantage of it! Poor Luciana. That business of wanting to get my own back – because I wanted to get back at Luciana for what had been done to me when mama, papa, Lita, didn't hug me – that business of wanting to get back at someone, I don't know if that leads . . . (leads?) Is "leads" what I want to say? "Leads to somewhere?" But who cares? The important thing is that I needed to get back at Luciana and I did. I'm not saying that I did wrong. I was done wrong. That's for sure. I am done wrong. Because it seems that several times in my life I've paid back the love that's been offered me with hatred. And hatred, boy, hatred is fire. But, is that really what it is? I don't know. I don't know what it is.

I'm going back to Tijucopapo because I want to see if I do know. I had to leave. Now on my road there are babassu palms and lots of shacks. Last night I dreamed of Luciana. I heard the cry of screech owls in the forest. It was a cruel dream. I'm not quite sure why I'm out here, on the move: maybe it's because of my cruelty. I want to see flowers.

Luciana was my first step into the messing up of my self.

What frightened me was my cruelty.

Could I have been as perverse as Severina Podre, Rotten Severina? Rotten Severina, a black boy there on our street, a dirty boy, and a little devil as they used to say, was so perverse that his mother, Mrs. Odete, would tie him up all day long to a tree trunk and beat him. He was called Severino but he seemed to be such a *thing* that they nicknamed him Rotten Severina. I don't know what it was he did that was so diabolical, I only know that was his reputation and he got a beating almost every day and howled like a wild beast. One day he bawled so much that papa left the house in irritation, me behind him, and knocked at Mrs. Odete's house asking if she wanted to kill the kid, saying that you didn't beat up on a kid like that. That it was cruel, inhuman.

Papa stupefied me maybe three times with bursts of kindness like that. But I was never really able to like him. Not that. And it was all his fault that I am almost turning into a Rotten Severina.

Because secretly, deep down inside, I used to admire and watch Severino. He always went by like a fierce silent animal. He didn't play with anyone, nobody played with him. He was someone who had succeeded. Who didn't need to ask anybody for anything. Who was even capable of playing alone. I recognized something in him.

I recognized that my cruelty was as great as Severino's. I would have to master it so as not to be an animal. So as to play with my group and be their leader. There was a rumor that Severino had already stabbed a man. But Severino was such a little boy. I'd have to master my cruelty before I ended up killing a person like Luciana. Before I terminally embittered a docile nature like Luciana's.

But one day I'll get in touch with Luciana again. I'll pick up the phone and dial:

"Hello, Luciana? Hi, Luciana. It's me, Risia. Risia. Yeah, listen, I'm calling to tell you that I know you're happy and that's nice. You are happy, aren't you? That's right, I could tell. Listen, I want to let you know that I am unhappy, and it's just what I deserve. I want you to enjoy knowing that I'm unhappy. I was really cruel to you. A big hug, Luciana. Good-bye."

Miss Penha sat down astonished in front of me, the letter in her hand, Luciana by her side, Luciana wiping the end of a sob in a wrinkled handkerchief. It was the most shameful day of my life.

My lips trembled in front of Miss Penha. I was ashamed. My head did not rise at her request. Miss Penha told me to raise my head, look Luciana in the eye and beg her pardon. My lips trembled at the first messing up of my heart:

18

"I'm sorry."

Why don't you just shove your forgiveness. And yours, Mr. Tom. And yours, Mr. Dick and Mr. Harry. If only I'd had a Miss Penha for every time I . . . But I didn't. That's why I didn't beg your pardon, Mr. What's-your-name.

6

Now I'm sitting on a boulder thinking that I really have to leave because that's the way I am. Because I am, among other things, a person who didn't know how to ask people's pardon. And don't let them think that I'm making myself out to be in the right. On the contrary, I'm constantly having to justify myself to myself. And I haven't any courage. What I am is just a big liar. Once, at the end of a day, I threw myself onto my bed and said to myself:

"Well, today was a day full of big lies, wouldn't you agree?"

I am not, in truth, a person who starts anything. Beginnings discourage me because I rarely believe in them. But I have a power for finishing that really impresses me. Even my desires sometimes get confused. I don't know if I really want to eat, for example. There's some sort of desire there but it might not be for eating. It might be a desire to not eat. Or it might be thirst. It's not a hungry desire. It's a thirsty desire.

It was very hot up there in Recife at midday, on the road to school. People went by:

"How are you?"

"As well as can be expected," I used to reckon the reply should be.

Ever since that road to school I am that sort of person, with no courage for anything. A person who doesn't know if she's going to school dead of thirst or if she will ever make anything out of life. I don't know if I'm going to school or if I'm making anything out of my life. Only if I'm marching in the parade. March in the parade . . . If I could still march in the parade as I used to on the seventh of September at school . . . The big drum pounding dum de dum up in front, Nema. Dum de dum, dum de dum, dum de dum. The trumpets pra pra pra tuning up for a fanfare that would shatter the dishes, the drums on the march, me in my gala uniform – shiny, glittering satin, and a beret – following the troop at a sharp trot. I trotted proud of myself. I need to do things that leave me proud of myself like that. Even though deep down I was marching with a tiny feeling of resentment that I couldn't be the drum majorette.

What frightens me is that some people are happier than others . . . I, for example, never could be the majorette that I was dying with desire to be. Brother Jorge and Sister Naninha, Nema's parents, were so happy back there in their life with just the two of them, always agreeing with each other about everything, and believing in the same God, and so on. Mama and papa were hellish. Papa betrayed mama with Analices, mama was a poor wretch, given away, pregnant, skinny, apathetic. Papa was an atheist, mama a believer. What came from them were unhappiness and death. Or maybe it was just me, the idiot.

And moreover, they used to throw stones at me in São Paulo, those sons of a bitch in the street. I had to get away.

I had to get away before I became completely crazy. It's incredible how things can make me crazy.

And among other things, I am a person who, like everyone else has been, is only going to have been. That drives me crazy. At the end of it all, I'm only going to have been. And not even ten parades beneath the glitter of satin and the brilliance of sequins will change the fact of my only having been, like everybody else. That makes me completely crazy. It anguishes me. Death completely anguishes me. Eternity and sacredness and power over time – the things that would make me different – I am not going to achieve them. What anguishes me about death is not what it implies, but what it leaves behind as absence. So, just imagine that I lost the love of a man. And, Nema, I separated from you, and I didn't remain in your arms, on that day in 1969.

I lost the love of a man, Nema, and you alone must know what that means to me. I'm dying yet not dying. I went five hundred thousand miles weeping from death and fear. And from anger because I didn't know who had done this to me. I am leaving in order to ask, in order to find out. I'm not going to ask. I'm going to find out. I'm going to make it.

I already experienced a few moments when I wanted to ask: "Why were you ever born, mama? Why on earth?"

Because, if you'd never been born, I could play, I would never have to leave off playing the whole afternoon because of you oppressing me. I wouldn't need to sort out your quarrels with papa. Nor amuse myself eating worms so as to vomit up my innards today.

Why do I need to know that you were given away and that you don't have a mother? That makes me feel an enormous pity for you. And why (why didn't you just shut your mouth, mama?) why do I need to know that you were betrayed right at home by auntie?

You know, you should have just shut your mouth, mama.

Papa! I ought to have killed you one day. Can you hear me, papa? One day, I ought to have killed you.

I had to leave home. I don't know what I'm doing out here. But I think it's so I can see if I'm making something of my life, which was marked by certain facts like auntie and papa betraying mama. But I think it's to see what's left of everything I used to be – me as a little girl, the street I lived on, my torturous memories.

I have to admit it's frightful that auntie and papa . . . Auntie and papa, I don't know how they did it, I don't know if it happened in bed . . . that they betrayed mama, the twit. Auntie used to be Ilsa. When she was a little girl she was so naughty that she ate salt as a punishment, until her mouth broke out in blisters and her stomach split open. Because she was caught smoking. It happened at Poti, the small moon-village where I was born and where those crazy things like auntie were born. I have to say it's difficult to think about her as Ilsa, because nowadays she wanders drunkenly around out there somewhere, a maid in some rich people's house, a savage servant, a drop of alcohol, a glass of wine, a laugh inside a sob – and there's nothing I can do for her. And then again . . . auntie betrayed mama and that's a shit. A shit because . . . That's a shit because I used to love auntie. I loved her with a strength I didn't feel for mama. Every afternoon, I would go to wait for auntie on the corner, wait for her to go by on the way home from the cafeteria at Varig where she worked. Auntie always used to bring a dessert, or a starter, from the meals on the plane. From the meals on the plane . . . Well, once I was eating in the plane on the way to Recife and I remembered auntie and myself as a little girl and teardrops fell and soaked the rolls in my dinner and I sobbed so hard that I almost vomited. So, now I am a person who goes around eating the airplane meals from the Varig cafeteria, the ones auntie used to prepare. And she, auntie, is now a savage alcoholic domesticated in the house of some rich people and I can do nothing about it except look at her helplessly and say what's left over from all the rest:

"So, you betrayed mama."

It was Poti, the moon-town where I was born and where those crazy women like auntie, or those wretched women like mama, were born, given away on a moonlit night by my grandmother, a heavy Negress, and who would later on be women with no mother nor siblings, strays, women so without anything, women so nothing. It was at Poti, and my mother was the adopted daughter of Sister Lourdes, auntie's mother. My mother had lost all contact with the truth of herself. Mama's last native link died out with the rays of the moon on the moonlit night when she was given away. Everything about mama is adopted and adoptive. My mother has no origins; in reality, my mother doesn't exist. I don't know if my mother ever was born.

7

But my mother was born, and it was in Tijucopapo. Sometimes I confuse the towns, saying that it was in Poti that those women who were given away like my mother were born. But what happens is that everything is so moonshone that all of a sudden I become moonstruck. Oh, if only I had it in me to not talk about anything. I wish I could shut up for days at a time. Oh, if I were at least able to talk in a foreign language. Oh, if only I could only grunt. Oh, if only I could be an animal. If I could be an animal I would be a mare, a mare that would launch herself at top speed, plucking up clods of soggy country mud or kicking up dust from the dry earth in the mountains. And that's how I would forget, God, that I lost the love of a man. I would forget that one day I sat at a table in a bar and hurt a man. Although I didn't want to hurt him. But he got hurt and died. And I traveled five hundred thousand miles trying to be the mare, which I'm still trying to be and still, right till now, not succeeding at. Today I am, among other things, a woman who tried to be a mare and didn't succeed.

It was in Poti, a moon-town, where I was born and where I know my grandfather was an Indian. Sometimes I look at myself in the mirror and I tell myself I come from Indians and blacks, darkskinned people, and I feel like a tree, I feel rooted, a manioc plant coming out of the ground. Then I remember that I am nothing. That I'm a person with hatred, almost a Rotten Severina, lunatic, moonshone, moonstruck, in a state of drunkenness without ever having touched a drop. And drinking reminds me of auntie. That's when I draw back from the mirror and I know I am a person assailed by tormenting memories.

When I learned, later on, that auntie had betrayed mama, auntie's hair had already been cut, it was no longer the long, thick black Indian tresses that I loved to play with when auntie came by the house every evening. Auntie herself never again had that serenity, that dignity of a person in whom I believed. In fact, starting with papa and mama, everyone lost their dignity for me. I no longer trusted, I no longer believed. And to no longer believe, to no longer trust, that burns you up, boy. Not even auntie could keep the bitterness from her face when I used to stare at it so as to avoid staring at mama's. When I knew the truth, auntie had already become the drunkard and the marginal person that she is able to be. Being marginal is for those who are able to.

When I remember – I am a person whose hellish memories prod at the rump of the mare that I'm not – when I remember that auntie became an alcoholic and veered toward the edges of life for the loss of the love of a man, I tremble. I'm afraid. My stomach churns.

The day of the greatest shame in my life was the day on which Miss Penha got hold of the letter I wrote to Luciana. I was used to doing and saying whatever I liked to people . . . But . . . But people used to do whatever they liked to me too, and that made me frightened and dumbstruck, frightened from wanting another language, anguished from wanting to be a whinnying mare so as to avoid being a woman who weeps her innards up because she has lost the love of a man.

24

People, boy, are hellfire. From the deepest pits of hell. People shatter me, that's all I know.

But I love people.

8

I'm dying but not dying because of those things that I know about life and about people, but I love people.

So be it – I'm dying but I'm not quite dead.

When mama married papa, auntie left home and went to live with them because auntie always had that sort of temperament: rebellious, wild and free, the temperament of a girl who learned how to smoke very young – and to smoke in Poti, the back of beyond – and then, she was the daughter of a believing mother, Sister Lourdes, and then, besides all that, she was a woman. Auntie was a scandal. But auntie was wise. She was the woman I would go to wait for on the corner every afternoon, as she came home from work bringing sweets to her nieces and nephews. How could I ever have imagined that auntie was betraying mama? If I had known it at the time, I would have killed her. Yes, I would. Or maybe not. Because I always said I would take a long knife or a sickle and kill Analice – my father's woman – the day I met her. I would loudly proclaim my hatred of Analice and people laughed at my bravery. Mama laughed, and Julieta and Ruth and Lita. People laughed, but they seemed to trust in my hateful bravery. People decided to trust in me, since they mistrusted their own selves. People decided to leave, subtly, to my account what didn't fit onto theirs. Mama, for example, thrust the weight of her pregnant world into my hands. Deep down, people really wanted me to kill Analice. People pulverized me. Only

Nema contradicted me, only Nema saw through me. And when I preached that way, justifying murder, Nema would give a shrug of doubt and disapproval:

"You're such a child."

Nema would always remind me that I was a child and always called me a child.

Until the day we met, Analice and I. Papa had bought a butcher's shop. Around that time I occasionally even had dreams of papa hanging from the hooks ready to be sold: loin, belly, tripes, tail. I was bloodthirsty. But I was such a child. When I got to the butcher's shop with mama, Analice was seated at the cash register. Mama and I recognized her for her blond hair. The only thing we knew about Analice was that she had blond hair. And that's what we saw. Analice was a blonde and even today I can't stand blond hair. My heart exploded into heavy thuds when I saw the great possibility in that being her, then: Analice, the blonde with the white skin, with the painted face, with the lipstick, the one with the makeup. My heart burst like a clock chiming the zero hour, the time between day and night that marked the encounter. Or the point where light and dark cross over. My heart burst for mama. There was a quick verbal exchange:

"Who are you?"

"I'm Analice. Who are you?"

"I'm Adelaide, his wife . . ."

"Oh."

"You shameless hussy, you whore, you tart, you devil . . ."

And mama had an attack and fell half fainting at my side. And my sickle, my hatchet, my butcher's knife? I tried to hold mama tight, my heart shattered, my braids choking my throat in a lump that finally burst into a sob, a sob like never before, a sob like the very . . . like you wouldn't believe. So where was all my

26

bravado now? I hadn't killed Analice. From that day on, when I appeared on the street the women jeered at me, mocked me openly, the women chopped me into pieces with sickles and hatchets. Had I been afraid of the blonde, then? It was the second day of the greatest shame in my life. It was the second shattering of my self.

No, I don't know if I would have killed my aunt. I haven't killed anyone. I have no courage. My strength, my anguish for vengeance, the need to avenge, doesn't take me very far, doesn't take me to a photo of me on a poster saying: **"Wanted: for parricide,"** papa. You're in luck. You're lucky I didn't have the strength to transform myself into an outsider and kill you. I only have the strength of a weakling. I'm delicate and fragile. And, moreover, it's my aunt I owe for having stanched the blood flowing from my navel when I was just born. They cut the umbilical cord wrong that linked me to my mother and I almost died of a hemorrhage in the night. It was auntie who saved me. It was in Poti, I was born at home and without a doctor. It was night and everyone was asleep in the house where I, newly born, wailed over the pain in my blood-soaked navel. Auntie took care of me and I'm alive today. That's what she always throws in my face when she's drunk. Auntie cries a lot when she is drunk. Because auntie lost the love of a man. Auntie loved a man who left her and went off to the Amazon. Auntie couldn't get over it and drinks glass after glass of pure alcohol and gets drunk, and works, like a savage, as a maid in a rich people's house. Auntie cut her hair and changed her face into bitterness. Auntie betrayed mama and there is no more waiting on the corner at the end of the afternoon, no more me and my child's life. Today I travel in Varig's airplanes.

9

I'm dying a slow death over these things I discover about life.

On the day of the second shattering of my self, the day I didn't kill Analice, I woke up stammering. And for a long time as a little girl I was a stammerer and skinny. The story of my stammering is long and sad. It's really horrible to be poor because you can suddenly become a stammerer or a skinny thing. The story of my skinniness . . . I was so skinny that they called me Risia Popeye. When mama told us about papa and auntie, I started stammering again. Now I don't stammer any longer, now I just get completely dumb or I talk directly in a foreign language. Or I leave straight away. But not being able to talk, being a stammerer, is a real incision, it's the very sign of a rupture, it's the greatest fright of all. Being a stammerer, then, made me shut up a lot. I became truly dumb.

But I feel that I need to leave off talking nonsense, because getting stuck in remembering my stammering is nonsense and vile. Leaving off nonsense, then, since every stammering individual is also a feeble spindleshanks, and I can't stand such weaklings like that, so leaving off all the nonsense, I shall speak, Nema, about what Sundays are like in São Paulo. There's something in me that has to do with Sundays, Nema. I hate Sundays because it was on a Sunday that I lost the love of a man. And Sunday changed back to being a total calm again where nothing ever happened. Where everything went on hold. But it was on Sundays that the worst torments happened, and the worst memories remained.

Nema, I lost the love of a man. Help me, please. What could I do on a Sunday? I wasn't even dirt dirty enough to take a bath, change into clean clothes and sit out there on the sidewalk waiting for the popcorn man to come by. Do you remember how in

Recife it was always on Sundays that the popcorn man came by, or the cotton-candy man, or the wafer vendor, with us sitting all clean on the sidewalk. What am I waiting for now, Nema?

And I would go out on the street and still hear a shout:

"Hey, goody-goody. There goes the old Bible-thumper. Miss Goody-goody!"

I threw a stone in one of their eyes. One day I almost split the head open of one of them, too. Then I took off at a run, crying. They know nothing about me. Go tell them they know nothing about me, Nema.

Is it possible that you can't hear me?

Today is Sunday and this Sunday it still dares to have the irony to be sunny. It's a sunny Sunday. I would prefer the sky to close over behind the dark clouds of a storm. That way I could cry under the rain. It's easier to cry with the rain.

My feelings are often like the rain – damp and dripping. Feelings that have been wept through, thick tears over the nature in this world that seems to me to be so cruel, a nature that doesn't wash clean, which not even the rain washes clean. So, if it were raining out there, with me watching out of the window, how else should I define these feelings except as if they were coming from the very summit of me, from my sky, to beat down in heavy drops at the very bottom of me, in my well? I overflow myself and get sad. I almost drown under this rainlike feeling. It runs out of my wet hair and clings to my clothes and pastes them onto my body, and leaves me crouching and soaked and trembling on a corner crossway with no shelter.

Whenever I was caught in heavy rain, I had a feeling propelling me like a little boat toward far-off places, as if to a place I've never been and need to reach to get away from this saturated melancholy that sloshes my feet through puddles of water. To places where the after-earth must be, that black earth trampled by grains of sand, that black earth that harbors the raindrops. Because the drops of my feelings, coming as they do from high altitudes, dance crazily, drunkenly, in search of a place to fall and stay. The wind slants them vertically over there and diagonally over here and I, I who am the size of a person and the weight of a person, I who don't have the slenderness nor the joyfulness of an earthworm, the only place I can give them to run is over my face, and that's how I make them cry on me.

They break at the altitude of my eyes and I am incapable of excavating the earth they search for. They shake me into sobs and I finish up being the ship that flaps its fragile paper as it slides over the red muddy furrows which I saw the rain open up on the street from behind my meager window. I saw the great strength of the raindrops that rend crevices in the earth – earth that yesterday had been so hard and dry – and strip fragments from a lump of clay I'm thinking about sculpting tomorrow.

But that feeling was a feeling – from when I was a little girl at the balcony of the window watching the rain – a feeling of: it's going to be very difficult to walk in all that rain, so I'll make little newspaper ships, I'll turn into a little newspaper ship and that's how I'll go, sailing away, propelling myself through the channels. So I make ships which I send straight out to trace routes for me and explore places for me that I, such a child, know nothing about nor what their name is, but I know that there are lots of them and they are as far away as the underworld must be. From my simple green window I threw little paper ships onto the eddies in the channels which started from the roots of the mango tree and stretched right through the yard until they crossed over the gateway and launched themselves into the street and into the world. And my teary sentiment was: where were those ships going that I couldn't go?

I had to remain at the window protected from the rain; if not papa would give me a beating.

In my agony, I leaned out through the window trying to find out if my anguish was the one I affirmed principally on those rainy days, since I believed that the little ships reached the street and therefore the world – since I believed that the street was the world – and I affirmed the smallness of my world which, after all, stopped right at the end of that street of dry earth. In a fit of temper, one day I made a hundred ships, a fleet, the Santa Maria, the Pinta, the Nina, mama, papa, Leide, Lúcia, Wilma, Mia, Ismael . . . A hundred ships, a fleet, a caravan of caravelles to carry me around the world which I was beginning to discover wasn't just that simple untruth of the end of my street. I was crazy. I was seven years old and all I knew about a city came from the Christmas before when they finally took me for a walk among the lights, and the people, and the shops in the center of Recife, and on tiptoe, astonished, from the bridge I saw – the river. It was only a glimpse but from that day on I had turned to living in a state of delusion: the landscape of my street had suddenly become impoverished in my eyes, with its small adobe houses, pot-bellied children, sad faces . . . And I wept over my weakness at the window during those days of heavy rain.

Not even the huge mango tree swaying immensely in the middle of the yard, my great fascination; not even the musical chorus of the frogs' croaking that came from the bushes to my ears in the night, ultimately the most uplifting and the most grandiose mystery of my childhood life; neither of those two presences could assuage the agony of a feeling entangled in filaments of rain, a sentimental-sobbing by a person who doesn't leave but sends herself off in boats to explore the other side of the seas which was only a city of lights and a river; but a person I could never find, because of papa and mama.

So, did that agony of mine come from papa? I hated papa. I was seven years old and I hated papa. I tried to forget him by eating earth and shitting worms. But what could I do on rainy days? I hated papa because of what he represented: he represented the mixture that was my rainy feeling running tearfully down my face – my feeling that, moved by so much rain, turned into weeping – and my feeling that caused me to need rain and at the same time demanded rain from me, the rain that dares to penetrate the deep, steep dwellings of the grains of sand, the black earth.

For the day before that one (the day when I made a hundred ships, the day when I was a little girl watching the rain from the window), one day before that day, and those days were a succession of intensely rainy days in the month of July and wintertime, one day before, papa had left me under punishment and without lunch for having succumbed to my desire to be rain. It was the same time, around the beginning of the afternoon. Jonas went by on his bicycle on his way to get food for the pigs; he went by whistling, and his tucked-up trousers let me see his legs all sunburned from going to the beach so often. Damn it, Jonas was the first man I loved, and he was going by under my window on a rainy afternoon, soaked through and inviting me to go along with him. We would go right across the field, pass by the stables, cross by the mill and the fountain, me on the back holding on round his waist, the waist of a liberated man with a bicycle in the rain, the wind carrying us like boats to some place that wouldn't just end at the end of our street, it would go some streets further on, or to the other side of the field, the rain dropping drizzle onto our faces, the rain making us rain, the tin cans dangling from the handlebars banging against each other and clanging a clamor that was our music, he a boy and me a girl. Damn it, Jonas was the first man I loved and I jumped out of the window to meet him and to follow him. We went right across the field, passed by the stables, crossed by the mill and the fountain, me on the back holding on round his waist, the waist of a liberated man with a bicycle in the rain, the wind carrying us like a boat, to beyond the end of our street, to the other side of the field, other streets, the tin cans dangling from the handle-bars banging against each other making the clamor that was our boy-girl music, the rain dropping drizzle onto our faces, the rain making us rain, the rain making us rain, the rain irrainiating us . . .

Then papa, who was waiting for me on the verandah with his belt in his hand, papa almost wrung me out – I felt like a soaked rag – with a whipping which he called: a whipping for your run-ning away. And he left me with no lunch on the verandah, crying great drops of immense longing for mama who was in the mater-nity ward, the rain falling in drops on the surface of the earth, my clothes glued together with a deep sense of sadness for my trembling body, my hair dripping sobs, me squatting down in such sorrowful abandon that only the arms of mama can con-sole. The arms I'd never had. I cried like never before. I cried like the rain.

On the next day I went crazy and made a hundred boats that would carry me to . . . mama? Yes, because now I remember that my agony was perhaps over mama who was in the maternity ward and from whom that downpour, which was the means for carrying me to the end of the world, to the other side of the seas, from whom that downpour separated me then came back and spat in my face the fact that I was not her, never could be. I hated papa. And from the city came the news that the river had burst its banks; I remembered the city of lights, and the river in which I'd looked at myself from the bridge. The river was overflowing in the news, destroying whatever immensity the fearful croak-ing of the night frogs had had in my stormy eyes.

That was it then, from the mean little window through which I was watching the rain, my agony was for mama herself,

33

from whom papa had brought the news that, if it hadn't been inserted into the newspaper headline like the news of the river overflowing, had inserted itself somehow into my eyes: although they hardly knew how to read, they saw it, that news, with the same fatality which seemed to me to weigh down the black letters in the headlines of the newspapers I turned into ships: MAMA CROSSED THE RIVER CAPIBARIBE BY BOAT, OVERDUE FOR CHILDBIRTH.

So that city and its long concrete streets had also succumbed to the seductive call of the waters of a river which, in my mind, could only resemble Jonas. The river could only represent, for the fiery and burning city of Recife, what Jonas represented for me as he went by under my window with his legs on display.

The streets and the lights were flooded, and I hated papa because he was the messenger of the disturbing news. And I could scarcely believe that all that belly that mama bore throughout those months of rain (a narrow red tube and me in her shadow) would have brought her a half-dead son sneezing blood in a hemorrhage through his eyes. Though in some way that death was my revenge. On the day papa came with the news, I glared at him like a murderer:

"Damn you, everything that comes from you and mama is death."

I acted pretty much like a Rotten Severina. But I cried a lot when they told me that Ismael looked like me. I wanted him to live, I was sorry. Two days after he was born Ismael would die in the incubator drowned in blood.

As it rained, the river had overflowed in an attempt to wash the nature from that world that seemed to me to be so cruel that not even the rain could wash it clean. And mama, suffering from the pangs of the moment of childbirth, crossed in a paper boat

34

the muddied city that was mingling with the River Capibaribe, to get to a maternity ward sure to be full of lights.

Here now there is a huge rainbow, which I remember seeing also on the day mama returned home bellyless and skinny. It was the dry week, I was out in the street and I remember that a ship from my fleet appeared intact protected by a stone that I called a cliff; the others must have gone off to the high seas, or broken into pieces on the way. But that surviving ship was the last in the line of the fleet, the one on which I had painted in red letters: *Ismael.* I stooped down into the drying furrow and began to sculpt my first clay object of the spring: a doll.

10

In winter, when the mounds of sand and the red earth of the street turned into mud, I made mudballs and hurled them at the walls in a rage at mama. I wanted to be a mare so that I could let fly with my feet. Or else I would sculpt little pots or dolls as my toys. If papa arrived and saw me with dirty hands, I'd get a beating. Papa always saw me.

But today must be a Sunday of sunshine in São Paulo, that place I'm leaving from. And it's not a question of me not being rain. I'm still rain. The sun's only shining ironically. And, one night, at moonrise, I burst into laughter. Under the rising moon, a laugh.

One night it was a Saturday night and I was alone at the bedroom window listening to a piece of old French music. His blond hair, wafted on a breeze of remembrances, knocked at the door of my memory. I love him. Then the radio played "Alone Again, Naturally." I was alone at the bedroom window, naturally. And the moon opened itself wide and concave in the sky, like a laughing mouth.

One night I had written among the doings in my diary: "For the love of God, if only I could be alone, from such and such to such a such a time." Yet later on, Nema, I would be dying from the solitude left by his departure. And no one would come to see me. And I had already promised myself not to visit anyone again until they came to visit me. I would never be visited again. I would never be visited again.

I hate São Paulo.

"You only know how to say that you hate," Nema used to think. But what's the way for me to love, Nema? Tell me from wherever you are, you who abandoned me. Damn it, you left me stuck in the middle of the street, unchosen – apple or pear? – at the end of the afternoon. Damn it. Damn. Damn. Damn.

So I became, among other things, the sort of person who didn't know what to write in her diary about him or about people. My problem began when I went back home and didn't stay out in the world, Nema. One day I looked hard at myself in the mirror: I was suntanned and pretty, but I was looking at myself in search of some trace of how other people were seeing me, Nema. I wanted to see how I was being seen. Those were my visions and visages.

I had to leave. Had to.

It was as if things were on the threshold of things. I look at myself and I feel the fear with which I see myself. What will become of me? That's what I ask myself. And I try to give myself an answer so that it will be easier to leave. Nothing is clearly defined any more, nothing is a road without zigzags. Everything is confused. Because, what I would see in São Paulo, in my house, in my room, was the doll, a childhood doll, in my bed, with its arms eternally raised, its open hands outstretched in a dumb

rigidified interrogation: "Please, what am I supposed to do?"
And that's not the way a doll should be seen. A doll gets carried
in one's arms and that's that. I can't even find a way of seeing
without deforming the object seen. I use the word *thing* to define everything I love that's already so formless it no longer has a
name, or whose name was actually lost under the white dust of
what nobody talks about, and which later reappears in the form
of a thing.

The word *thing* is the correct undefinition of everything.

The word *thing* is the correct undefinition of everything.

The word *thing* is the correct undefinition of everything.

It makes one want to smoke dope and trip for eight solid
hours, said a young girl once in a troubled moment. What should
I do, I now ask, what should I do with all the hours of my life, in
that case, if they are all filled with troubles? It makes you want
to take a double dose and trip out all the time.

Dope, Nema. You can't imagine what that is. Drugs, nar-
cotics, marijuana, peyote. I should have tried some. I never did,
but people do smoke dope. I lost the love of Jonas and I should
have used peyote to turn into a mare. I could turn into any animal I wanted to. I should have taken drugs because I can't stand
this pain thing. It's the pain of my having lost Jonas. I'm dying
but not dying from so much pain. I should take some drugs so as
not to die. Oh, no. I don't want to die. I think I'm still able to
love. I'm still able to love. I don't want to die, Nema.

Peyote, Nema.

Nema a a a a a a a a a a . . .

Nema, it was December 1969. There was all the usual stuff
about it being the end of a year. The end of a year, Nema, and the
end of . . . Christmas . . . You know Christmas used to make me
sad, Nema. There was all the usual stuff about it being Christmas. I was messing around in the street and it was the end of the

afternoon. Night was already falling but softly still, with the lazy torpor of a summer evening. I was messing around playing as I did every evening, Nema. But the thing was, and you saw this for yourself, Nema, that evening they didn't light the street lights. It was darkening, it was dark. But I was playing. What was I playing at, Nema? Since you were the one who arrived. I didn't remember that I was due to leave on the next day, either. I had no idea what it would mean to leave.

I was playing at apple-or-pear. Was it apple-or-pear, Nema? Apple-or-pear? I was playing apple-or-pear:

> You shall pass, you shall pass.
> But the flag must stay here.
> If not the one at the front,
> Then the one that's in the rear.
> – Apple or pear?

And the other children were passing under the arch, Nema. While the one who replied to "apple or pear?" would stay with me or not. Was I apple or was I pear, Nema? One of them would stay with me, or not, Nema. What sort of a flag is it that flies when people choose not to stay with us and leave, Nema? What sort of a flag is it that will stay? Does the flag have to stay, Nema?

Nema, it's the beginning of another year now, Nema. Back in São Paulo it seemed as if it was just getting late, and it seemed as if they had torn up the lights in my street. To the point that I had to leave and be out here on the road.

So I was playing at apple-or-pear, Nema, and the next day you would be in Pedra Branca at the time of our departure. It was December 1969. And Pedra Branca, Nema? White stone, lilywhite stone, pure stone. And the sugarcane, and the flour mill, and the river, and the horse? Nema, goddess of my heaven, and what about the God I nodded off to in the church by mama's side? What about that God, Nema?

What am I here for? What can I do? Die?

It seems as though people don't die here, Nema. It seems as though people just suffer a lot here. Nema, they made me suffer as only pure suffering can feel. I am a suffering, Nema.

Why? Why, Nema? But if it was in the evening, Nema, and the end of a year, and if you knew . . . And if there were no lights in the street, Nema. I was playing at apple-or-pear when you came with your suitcase. You came up behind me and went under the arch. And all the children laughed because you were very tall and almost undid the arch.

So there you were . . . Listen, you were so tall playing volley-ball. I had never seen anyone play volleyball, you were the first. And you took me over to your school, into that large yard, and I saw all the girls there, playing volleyball, and you too punching the ball over the net. All my pride jumped with you each time you served.

My pride was you. You were tall and beautiful playing volley-ball. And you were dating Bué behind your father's back. You were brave. What you meant to me was: if it were possible for you to be like you were, then I would be too. One day I would be. So, being was possible. I should admit it now, after so many years have gone by, that I loved you. That I loved you even though the words I spoke were of hatred. For once you told me:

"You always say that you hate."

Nema a a a a a a a a a a . . .

Nema, it's the beginning of a year now and I need to say that I hate because if I don't I die. Nema, I need to say that I hate be-cause love turns me into a state of suffering that drives me crazy.

That's why I left, Nema. If it hadn't been for that afternoon, if it hadn't been for you not embracing me forever back there. I wouldn't have left, Nema. I wouldn't have left.

But I loved you, Nema. If you could be, I might be – that was what I clung on to. And at school, in my schoolbook, I read and reread a poem which reminded me of you, and went:

> Ema and seriema
> Ema and seriema
> Mermaid and bird
> Is Nema and Noemi

Nema.

There were drawings of birds, emus and seriemas browsing steep and tall like you on the edge of the beach.

But if it was the end of the afternoon, Nema, and the end of a year, and if you knew . . .

Why you? Remember, you came under the arch of my apple-or-pear, and turning to face me, you said:

"I'm going to Pedra now. I won't be around tomorrow at the time you all leave. I came to tell you good-bye."

"Good-bye," I said fiercely.

"Won't you give me a hug?"

And you hugged me. A hug. You hugged me a hug. Suddenly I . . . So, I . . . was hugged. It was my first hug. And maybe your third or fourth. Papa and mama had never hugged me.

Nema, you held me too strongly in those great volleyball-player's arms. How old were you, Nema? I felt so little. You held me close to your breast and wept on my shoulder. You wept on my shoulder, Nema. Did I weep on yours?

> Nema,
> Ema steep and emusical.
> And the sea, Nema, the beaches, seriema?
> Nema and Noemi.

And you hugged me a hug. You hugged me a hug. I was suddenly half-smothered in your arms, and half saying to you:

"It won't be as bad as all that . . ."

And you hugging me even more, pressing me closer, then let me go, alarming me with a face full of tears.

"It won't be as bad as all that, will it?" I was begging you.

You stood me on my feet.

"Please hug me again, I don't want to go." I was almost begging you.

Then you went away.

Behind me the children had continued the song: "You shall pass, you shall pass."

I stood fast in the middle of the street till you disappeared around the corner.

Nema.

You should have stayed with me in your arms. Why didn't you stay, Nema? And I wouldn't have come on this journey. You knew what it would be like here. Your arms, Nema. Your hug.

What sort of a flag is it that flies when people choose not to stay with us, and leave? What sort of a flag is it that will stay? Should the flag stay, Nema?

What can I do, Nema? Die? But it seems that people don't even die here. What can I be? What fruit? An apple? A pear? The fruit of love, am I not a tree that bears it? Am I just a weed? Tell me what I am, Nema a a a a a a a a a a . . .?

So it would seem that "You shall pass" is a hymn of vengeance and glory that has followed all along the road love made in my direction. You shall pass – and I just can't stand that pain, Nema. You shall pass, and I hate you. For your arms are what I need. I just want you to stay, and apples and pears shall be yours. And you would never ever have to choose again. I have both apples and pears to give to you.

If I want to I go out in the rain, Nema. If I want to I play in the sand. If I want to I suck pitomba fruits, I climb onto the table. If I want to I do what I want, Nema. Do you remember when mama left you to take care of us? I was a stubborn little pest, but you liked to hear me say I could do anything. But what is it that people want in São Paulo, Nema? I already asked people. Nobody does anything, nobody wants to do anything. It doesn't rain there, there's no sand, there're no pitombas. There, even if I wanted to, I can't do things, Nema. There, sometimes, Nema, in the streets as evening falls there, I stop there in the middle of the median waiting for the cars to pass, indifferent and forlorn, and trying to tell myself I'm a whore: I'm a whore, take me anywhere you want to. For that's the only way I might surrender to the full and total ease that giving my own body implies: without pride, without dignity, without love, without pain. Because I cannot handle love body and soul. Love in the soul pierces my soul. And a bleeding soul is vampirism. And a vampire, you know, Nema, is an unhappy creature that only knows how to make victims out of love. Fluttering in black capes in the middle of the night. Victims of love. The unlucky ones, Nema.

Nema.
Nema and Noemi.
Mermaid and ema.
Ema.
Nema.

What can I do? Talk to you in this hour of suffering? Talk to someone who's not even you any longer? Talk to others who aren't you? So that they'll know? The ones who never even noticed? The same ones who pass under my arch today? Is that all I've got left? At the moment of suffering, to confess? In fact, does the confession have to be mine? I was only playing apple-or-pear. It was the lights that didn't light up.

And from here you don't hear me.

It was awful, Nema. It was worse, as worse as it would ever be. Nema a a a a a a a a a . . .

I didn't weep on your shoulder. I wept when the bus went by the Boa Viagem beach.

Mermaid and Ema.

Nema, seriema.

11

When I arrive there, it's certain that I'll have seen flowers, I want to see red flowers, when I get there after having gone through beds of flowers in the middle of the fields, I'm going to write the letter in English and send it.

My mother was born.

I'm going to talk about when and how it was that my mother was born, before it gets too late. Nema and Ruth were sisters and they were the persons who took me out on walks. In Lita's house, at the back of Lita's house, stood a guava tree. Julieta had everything rich people have. Auntie drinks glassfuls of pure alcohol. Sister Naninha, the mother of Ruth and Nema, only knows the road that leads to the church: the exception in the midst of all the Anas, the whores. Sister Lourdes is a believer and a sufferer because auntie, her daughter, became a drunkard and an outsider. My grandmother gave my mother away on a moonlit night. Poti is the moon-town where I was born. I, who fly in Varig's airplanes.

I'm going to tell you something.

The darkening of evening is the outflow for all absences. It's the wind blowing nostalgia and pain. I don't know how I haven't died yet. But I'm on the brink of death. And I believe that it's nightfall itself that makes me flow out to die, a little bit each evening.

I feel as if I'm getting closer to the very end. The beginning stayed back there behind a whole range of mountain ranges. How do I connect the one with the other?

My mother was born. I have a beginning there.

My mother was born.

Oh, getting there is so tiring. How many thousands of miles have I gone? Two hundred and fifty? How much more is there to go? On my road there are babassu palms and shacks. I am a woman traveling alone on the highway.

Sometimes I stop on a bridge or by a boulder, I sit down on the edge and strum a bit of music on the guitar I'm carrying, or I try out some different colors with my wax crayons on a landscape.

At times I need to stop.

The fact is that here am I, a woman alone on the highway. My beginning stayed back there behind a whole range of mountain ranges. I had to come. I left because there was no place at all for me to fit into. I left because the man who loved me and whom I loved decided to die and I was left to face many dangers. I moved around from house to house never knowing where to put myself. I left because I almost lose my speech in the big city. Because my house, on Sundays, was completely crazy. It was a day of silence. Everyone would be at home, on their day off. And it was exactly the day on which dumbness was intensified. On Sundays, the people in my house never spoke to each other. Completely crazy. São Paulo. I had to leave and move on. Here I'm treading out my own path on the earth. There are palm trees and cane fields. The canefield leaps over the hills, comes back down, then shows up again in the distance, light green. Everything is green color as I walk through the brush that borders the road. When I get tired, I take my crayons and paint other colors onto the landscape that I draw on white paper. Only the cane field is very green. This is where I'm traveling.

But first: the women of Tijucopapo. The birth of my mother. These scraps of memories startle my soul at every moment. They prick the mare's rump I would so much love to have. The women of Tijucopapo, before it gets too late. Every thought reminds me of the women of Tijucopapo. I'm going to introduce people to the women of . . . , before I lose the track. Before I lose the track: the women of. Colored in red in many shades. I will. Yes. I know how to draw, too. How to draw a mud bomb that burst into two around me and sprayed into my eyes, my tears, and into my mother around the birthsack. And I was born. I am made of filthy mud. And tears. Once upon a time, where the beach turns into mud, at Tijucopapo, my mother was born. I am made of mud that is black with earth. I am slippery. Every thought, every day, reminds me of the women of Tijucopapo. In a quaking, in a thrashing that I can never get beyond, I never get beyond. In a shuddering fit that, if I'd already got there, would mount me on a horse and send me off like a shot in search of the explanation that might lie where the beach meets the mud, the black tijuco clay. Where those women came from, my heritage, women made of the substance of *tijuco*, thick-haired, dragging on their horses' manes, straddling the beasts bareback, amazons. Once upon a night, upon a time, my mother was born in the heart of a swamp. In a mud plain. Women like my mother bear the mark of certain women who take off to face the world straddling their horses, amazons, defending themselves no one knows exactly from what, except, as we know, from love. The only thing that's known is that love makes them suffer. The only thing that's known is that love makes them betrayed. They are amazons on horseback coming to make their mark on the tijucopapo, where everything's a mire. The women of tijuco-papo: horseshoes. The women of Tijucopapo: it's as if so little remains of everything; and it's as if so much remains when it turns itself into a heritage. The women of Tijucopapo: they are me with my mark of mud, I who emerged, a mud creature, a worm, where the beach meets the mud.

The women of Tijucopapo: yes. I'm coming. I'm slippery. Lita. When I remember Lita. When I remember my aunt. When I remember Lita. When the days stretched out, unbearably hot for days and months at a time, and Recife was catching fire, Lita would group together the faithful in the church to sing for "The Grace of Rain":

> The grace of rain
> We ask for rain, O Lord
> Send us plentiful rain
> Rain from the Consoler.

But at the bottom of Lita's yard stood a red guava tree, open-mouthed, gums exposed.

12

But what good does it do me to avoid things? I no longer have the beginning I think I have. My beginning got lost many mountains ago, I'm not going to start anyone in anything. I don't know how to start things. I only know how to end things. But it's very diffi-cult to get to the end, too. I know that nothing remains of the be-ginning and I should place all my hopes in the ending. It would be easy if I weren't exactly in the middle. I'm in the middle, half-way. What good does it do me to avoid things? This is a nobody's road I've already traveled two hundred and fifty thousand miles on. And I'm here because I could no longer use the telephone. Because I couldn't talk any more. Because mine is a case of the loss of love. I was, once and for all, shattered into pieces. Unhappiness took a running jump at me, and smacked me right in the kisser. I can hardly believe it, I'm so stupid, an idiot. Sometimes I stop and lean on a stone or a tree along the way because I'm almost fainting from walking on in disbelief. Sons of a bitch. All of them. All of them who made me have to leave. Son of a bitch. You know, I loved that man and, all of a sudden . . .

And they shouldn't call me names in the middle of the street. What I am doesn't have a name. Not even Rotten Severina.

It's not possible . . . I'm leaving right now. I'm on the road again. It's the end of the afternoon. I'll spend the night in any shack where they open the door to me. I left home. I lost Jonas, the son of a bitch . . . No, no, I can't take it. Trying to be organized, positive, doesn't get me anywhere. I can curse, though. I need to curse against those tricks that annoy me, against those tugs that pull on my arm paying no attention that my arm is delicate, weak and fragile. My arm is still covered with all those red fingermarks.

Jonas died for me. Things weren't that bad. What came over him?

Avoiding things doesn't get me anywhere. The landscape of a flight is trees and stones and a few shacks and cattle grazing. Someone, a vegetable seller, crosses my path in the early morning. He goes by straddling a languid donkey, heading for the city. The landscape of a flight is winds and the sun of many days of walking and the nightly struggle among the roars and whistles of all the animals. I travel very fearfully.

I travel fearfully and I am exposed to every conceivable danger.

13

Once upon a time, just once, I lost the love of a man and set out on a route thousands of miles long weeping of death and fear. I cried like never before. I cried like you wouldn't believe.

The love of a man, I cried like a woman:

When you died, I'm going to write an elegy.

When you died the mornings are nights without moon. My desire as I get up, or don't get up, every day, is to not believe it:

"Did you die?"

And I don't believe you died.

No you?

You?

Without you it's a struggle to get up to believe. Did you die?

Me, I'm a hole, a hollow, a dryness, an emptiness. I'm the night in the morning. Will I never again have sunshine? The rain from such a gray sky hurts my face. Oh God, the ashen grayness of that death.

That death that comes, then, and doesn't go away? That comes fatally, finally.

When you died I'm going to write an elegy. If I believe it I can't get up.

When you died I'm going to look, in all my old photographs, for my smiles. Will I never laugh again?

When you died I weep my salt tears. And the sea breaks way out but I needed it to happen here inside me. And for me to swallow waves of water for this emptiness, hollow, dryness.

When you died I take off into the fields like a startled mare. And – ironically – I'm running once more with the freedom of my mare's legs. I no longer want the world or anyone. I sway my body, I toss my mane, I fan my tail. The field is green and infinite. That's the only way I save myself: by being in an infinite field where you are not the boundary; you were the boundary? What irony.

The green field stretches before me and I do somersaults when you died. I flail my arms and legs like a gymnast. I do leaps and acrobatics. When you died I need to live. My body.

But and mysoul? There's nothing to tow it away from the tempest your death aroused. But did you die?

You didn't die, you didn't die, you – did – n't – die.

I turn five cartwheels in the field in the name of your non-death.

Please, don't have died.

When you died I don't know if I hate you or if I hate life, that life that dares to keep me living while it kills you. Was it life that killed you? The same life that lives me on?

Me? No, it wasn't I who killed you. I might perhaps have wanted to hurt you. But kill, no. Never.

But if it's true that you died, then get out from under me once and for all. For this death of yours is my torment in life. It's me who's dying now. At least let me run around here in the field, myself: a mare with neither a stallion nor a foal. I don't want anyone any more nor the world.

On the day you died I picture you alive and even believe that you are watching me thinking of you here, creating you in the images of someone who didn't die.

You didn't die. You didn't die. You didn't die.

That isn't done to a person – dying.

But if you did die, leave me in peace. Don't show yourself to me. And go away once and for all. Don't hang around whispering to me (about what? about your death?) or spying on me through the keyhole.

That I can't stand.

That isn't done to a person – dying and not dying.

Oh, but you didn't die.

Please, don't have died.

After you I'm going to have to lilive. Just living isn't enough and nearly makes me die.

When you died, they ask me if I'm a monster, death.

Then I stick out my tongue, give them a banana and say:

"The monster is your mother, death."

When you died, what do I do with myself? Where do I put myself?

When you died I ask other men in the street:

"Hey you, guy, do you want to go with me?"

I almost ask. And I add:

"But you're not going to think of dying, I hope? If that's the case, I don't want you, man."

When you died I translate all the elegies.

Oh, but I love you.

Please, don't have died.

You didn't die. You didn't die. You didn't die.

When you died I don't forgive you because you preferred to die for me to staying with me.

And that isn't done to a person.

When you died, one day I'll phone you again:

"Hello. Is that you? Yes, it's Risia here. Did you die? Listen, I'm calling to tell you you are a big shit for having died. To tell you that dying – that just isn't done to a person. That you shouldn't have done that to me. That you are nearly killing me. That I'm on the brink of death. And that I really want to tell you to f . . . off. But then I . . . I'm . . . also dying with longing and I'm calling you just to ask you to, please, don't have died. Please, don't have died. Because I love you. Good-bye."

When you died, do I fix myself up with other men, or do I respect your death by going into mourning for a while? How long? Time. Time. Time. It's time itself that I can't stand. I can't bear time. Time is just one of two things: either it doesn't pass, or it passes by too fast. Will you make me a timetable, a frame, a clock, an alarm so I can move inside time? Because I'm not going to stand a time that's all fragmented, massive, monstrous, fearful, death. Tell me, "tomorrow," or "a month from now," but don't tell me "maybe." "Maybe" unleashes me into time and finishes me off. And don't ever tell me "never," either. "Never" defines a road, a road I don't want to take. "Never" is the road of death. I can't stand your death, man, coming here and falling heavy and hurtful into my hands. What do you think my hands are made of? Iron? Wood? Concrete? They are made of flesh, man. I am human, man. Do I need to shout that out loud? I am human. Can you hear me? I am human. My hands are made of the same flesh that two nails can drive through and pierce holes in on their way to the wood of the cross. My hands are made of flesh that bleeds blood; I'm human, man.

Oh God, I'm going to die.

When that man died, Nema, I'm going to die.

I'm not going to stand it when that man died.

What is it that kills me when that man died? Oh God, it's the love of mine for that man. Oh God, why don't you come to Earth? Listen, be a magician and give me back that man again. Go on now, give him back. Damn it, the Lord's magic is full of shit. His magic tricks come out all back to front. Instead of love, it's death that comes out of his black top hat.

14

So, do you think it's admissible, Nema, that a man do what he did to me?

That isn't done to a person, Nema – to not hug her and to leave her alone to finally confront that monster, death.

Shall we play at singing, Nema?

Nema used to play at singing with me. When I was a little girl I was happy sometimes. I invented thousands of games. I used to laugh a lot, too. When I played at singing I would always be Wanderleia singing "We are young." Now I speak English and I sing John Lennon:

> Mother
> You had me
> But I never had you
> I wanted you
> You didn't want me.

Mother, you had me but I never had you. And I wanted you, you never wanted me. Mother, you shitface. It's a little just so's you won't understand that I sing John Lennon. I want people to not understand. I'm going to talk in English:

> Mother, I sing John Lennon
> Father, I sing John Lennon
> Nema, I sing John Lennon.

And I sing of the hellishness of everything that exists. Look at me here: I'm the very devil, Old Nick, a black cat on a broomstick.

God, how I can curse.

I have a mania for cursing. I'm such a prattler, I rattle on with God and the devil himself about me myself.

I want this particular letter to go in English because English is the most alive language in the world. The other languages seem dead alongside English. Just imagine that even languages die . . . Dead languages exist. And – no – I – can't – stand – death. English is alive. Live! English is alive:

> Father,
> You left me
> But I never left you
> I needed you
> You didn't need me.

Father, you left me but I never left you. I needed you, you didn't need me. Father, you son of a bitch.

English is made of foreign stuff that fascinates me and separates me from all that closeness of sending a letter from me in the language of my own people, in my own language. I don't want them to know about me like that, so closely. I want them to not understand me. English gives me distance:

> So I
> I've just gotta tell you
> Good-bye.

So I just have to tell you good-bye, father, good-bye, mother, good-bye, everyone.

I left home because Sunday at my house was crazy. We were really poor. And there was that thing of one person deserting the other. We were alone, adoptees.

Today I'm on the way back to Tijucopapo, Nema.
Today I want to see Zana, Hozana, and have a kid in my belly

and three dragging at my skirt and live in that miserable sugar mill shantytown: just as long as what I have is enough love to give me strength and lead me into discovering. Today I'm on the way back to the cane fields, Nema. I'm going back to discover. I'm going back to make it.

15

And now I need to invent the dream that I'll dream tomorrow. Tomorrow I'll dream of . . . let me see . . . let me see . . . tomorrow I'll dream that he didn't die and that we are together throwing stones into the river at Pedra Branca. Tomorrow I'll dream that we are happy, he and I. The waterfall at Pedra Branca will draw itself completely inside my head, just as it really is, crystalline and turbulent. I'll do it at midday, my worst time, that way I'll stay for hours inside my dream. Midday will go by without my noticing it. These dreams give me relief. In these dreams I travel far away. I travel, I create real stories. When I wake up, I laugh at myself, look to see that no one's watching, and call myself an idiot. Idiots, inside that silence of theirs, must continually be creating long stories. I die of shame in case someone might know that I'm doing this. When the dream stops – and I never know what makes it stop or in which moment it stops – it's always horrible. Even if midday has already gone by. Tomorrow, when I wake up from the dream about him, I'll need to dream another straightaway otherwise I can't stand it. It'll be very sad to wake up knowing that he preferred to die on me rather than enter into my stories and go with me to Pedra Branca. Tomorrow, right after my dream of him, I'll dream that the world is a hellhole and in flames. That the world's catching fire. Revolution. Cosmic fire. The final judgment. And I'll spring up in fright and excitement. And I'll go out naked like a crazy woman, with my eyes popping out and an idiotic grin, shouting to the crowd to set itself on fire, and shouting to the burned-out rubbish of this world:

"Burn, damn you! Carbonize yourself, damn you! Have done with it, total out, damn you! Get lost, damn you!"

Nema, that's the way I do it, now that I'm here, so I can put up with midday. I get out my midday dream. Do you know when it was that I first dreamed? When it was 1969 and I first set foot in São Paulo. It was there in that city that I turned to needing to invent dreams. I turned to needing the world to come to an end.

I was forced to choose to leave. I'm painting a revolution in crayon colors.

When I was forced to choose which way I was to be, I opted for the way I knew best.

In that city I'm leaving from, that huge city of building sites and people and cars and garbage going by and city life-styles, the people are playing a losing game. Things do happen, and stories take place in their thousands, but stories also get lost in their thousands, they die right where they are born. Every person is a lost story.

In that city I'm leaving from, and those Sunday evenings with no popcorn man going by in the street, with no me in clean clothes sitting on the sidewalk waiting for the sugarcane vendor. Nothing, there's nothing left. I see the sky darken. I had to leave. I couldn't stand those evenings.

When I had to choose which way I should be, I opted for the way I know best: this unknown road. The thing is that, on this road, I can see the mornings being born. Not everything is the evening. Today, for example, it's morning time. Today is morning time. I got up to continue my journey on this road on my own. He died. But today is a day of calm because last night I didn't dream of him. When my dreams happen to be about him, the sun burns down from on high and leaves my entire body in a disturbed state that lasts for days. Or else it'll be raining and I go on my way saturated, almost done for, slipping on the mud, stumbling through the furrows like a newspaper boat launched by a child. He's always watching me in my dreams. I wake up with him in my head. By day he accompanies me in images that are amazingly real. Death is a shadow which ever afterwards will never let us go. If you can manage it, don't ever let anyone die.

But it was in that city I'm leaving from that I made myself into a woman. I'm leaving that city, as a woman. I don't deny that. A woman – I loved silent men and I loved talkative men. I loved men in the tepid darkness of the night. I mounted mountains of men. And my mother never even suspected it. I always felt very guilty when I'd face her the next day after spending the night in a hotel with a man. It was horrible knowing that yesterday I had betrayed her. There was no way she could know. There was no way my mother could know anything about anything. The only thing my mother used to know how to ask was if I'd eaten a proper lunch. Suddenly I had her in my hands – I knew more than she did. I'd come home anxious to see her, to talk to her, a huge sort of love for her was emerging in those hours of betrayal. And if I didn't find her at home? And if she didn't come back straight away? I was afraid of losing her as happened one Christmas in 1964 when she slowed down the whole of life itself in the city, pregnant, almost giving birth to Ismael in the street and only coming back on the very last bus, with me bursting into tears. So, once I used to burst into tears for my mother. But – good for me – every one of my days afterward, all my life since I was a little girl, used up half of their hours (twelve hours a day) in betraying my mother: from the sweets I ate hiding in the kitchen to the pill I took every night, in some hotel bed. I am a traitor, mama, hang me high.

What a joke.

A joke, because, damn it, why should I be to blame? If I were to blame, my mother is twice as much to blame as me.

So there. And on that note, I say good for me! Well done, for all the cheeky letters I've written up to now.

16

For the rest of my life I'll carry around the attitude of that revenge letter I wrote to Luciana. And the remorse. For every letter of mine, someone writes a song to Luciana's distress until my ears ache with remorse and I start to cry. Oh, if I could only make a phone call. I'll carry that attitude around for ever, as I did at Manjopi. Manjopi, my first experience in a group, a disaster. That revenge attitude in a letter to Luciana is what makes me a person who withdraws, a person who's inhibited, a person who's worth nothing. Nothing. However much people may be different from one another, nothing makes them so different among themselves as when I see that I in no way resemble them. And that makes me uneasy. I can't even make a telephone call. I even have to beat a retreat. I'm walking out here along a road of babassu palms and shacks under a barren sun. I can see a whole range of mountain ranges but I don't know how many thousands of miles I've gone. Two hundred and fifty? That many? If only I could make a phone call. My first group experience took place in Manjopi and I was a little girl. Everything happened in that same time when I was a little girl. All the rest, life, is redundant. Early on, early, I learned of the other side people have, a side that runs off slippery like mud. Early, very early on, in the early morning, in what existed of the very dawn of my life. And ever since then I've been lost, a lost person who doesn't look like herself, who can only retreat. I . . . but sometimes I get into such a fury, into such an enormous revolt against what people did to me, that it wouldn't take much for me to kill one of them. They shattered me into pieces. It makes me so enraged that I call them all sons of a bitch. Sons of a bitch. Fish faces. Encephalitics. And, I should add, shamelessness does exist. It exists because I, it was I, it was I who discovered that particular disaster. They forced me to discover it. Shamelessness exists because I discovered it in them with my own pure eyes, with the eyes of the morning of my life. They shattered me. And they still go around back there saying that I'm not this, I'm not that, I don't do this, I don't do that, the only thing I care about is myself, and so on and so on about me, that is, about myself. So I am a bit of everything. I'm everything. Encephalitics, sons of a bitch.

I'll never disrespect the little girl that exists inside me. The little girl that exists inside me is seated on a throne. My childhood was huge, immeasurably huge; there were days when it weighed down my stomach and almost made me vomit. There were nights when my childhood shoved me out of bed and prevented me from sleeping with it. Space. There is no space that a childhood fills full. A childhood is anxieties. A childhood doesn't fill any space, it doesn't fit, it spreads out into what I am right up until now, into what I'll always be.

Manjopi, shame of my life. Manjopi, the reflex of my complexes. The pupils of the third year at school all went on an outing to Manjopi. The first time I was going out with other people who were not mama, Nema, or Ruth. With classmates from school. Manjopi had swimming pools and picnic tables. Broad green grassy spaces and a carousel. I don't know why I had to go.

For I always used to die of shame when people saw me like that, close to. So much so that I was silent throughout the entire journey in the bus, dying from rage at Luciana, who in those hours when I needed her wasn't coming to talk with me. In those hours she didn't come, the stupid sluggard. And I didn't have the minimum resolve needed to strike up a conversation with anyone at all, not even with Libânia. I was dying with shame of her especially. I was traveling dead with shame, squashed against the window seat. I shouldn't have come along, I had stuck myself in where I shouldn't have been. It wasn't my environment. I was incapable of even opening my mouth. If I opened my mouth I would stammer – and that would be the final stroke of shame. I was poor. I felt ugly. I was so skinny in front of the girls. I really was the girlfriend of Popeye. When television sets arrived in our street, the children nicknamed me "Popeye's scarecrow." Toothpick. Olive Oyl. The one who should have been eating the spinach. I told them to fuck off, sent them to hell, back to the bitch that gave them birth. I . . . but in Manjopi I learned how really skinny my legs were. In Manjopi I learned about how different I was. Manjopi – my hair looked like a hangman's ropes kneaded with the brilliantine mama put on it and that the sun melted at midday. My hair wasn't smooth like Libânia's or Maisa's. I had coarse hair. I had skinny legs. The perfect blueness of the swimming pool intimidated me even though I used to beat my cousins at swimming races in the river at Pedra Branca and I used to dive through the steepest waves that ducked us at the beach. On top of all the rest, the girls were the daughters of rich sergeants. I was poor and my mother was a believer. I was a scholarship student in a class of plump pink girls who smacked kisses at Miss Penha's face. Such complete intimacy with Miss Penha. Kisses. I think I'd never kissed anyone. In Manjopi I spent hour after hour imagining what it would be like to kiss Miss Penha's pretty face.

Miss Penha was elegant, pale, and slender. The girls, the sergeants' daughters, pink and plump, were playing like little kids and came running up to smack kisses onto Miss Penha's face. I remained, through the whole of Manjopi, in a state of desire. I remained with the desire to play and to kiss Miss Penha's face. I remained in a corner until the picnic was over. I didn't play even once at Manjopi. When I don't play I die. In Manjopi I died a little. Manjopi. Big shit. I hadn't made it. How many Manjopis did I have to spend before I made it to where I am today – capable of arranging a face that can put up with a party with sergeants' daughters? In the end, that's the shit you get, the shit of a face that can put up with anything. Because if you don't, you become an animal. You have to go to the most diverse sorts of parties, so you don't turn into an animal. And as for me, as I'm on the edge shitting with fright, I arrange the most diverse faces for the most diverse picnic parties. And anyway, you always get a bit of a laugh at parties. You can always mimic somebody's facial twitch, somebody else's idiocies, you can always drink a little alcohol, you can always live it up a little. There were days when I gave everything to go to a party. Sure, parties are good, who says they're not?

And anyway, parties belong to fortune's little darlings. You always eat well, you always drink whole Coca-Colas. Who doesn't love fortune's little darlings? Me, I hate them. There are times when I hate fortune's little darlings because I don't know how to understand those sorts of people who never ate earth nor shat worms. People who were never hungry or thirsty. People who always sat their ass down on a carpet or a cushion. Fat pink people. Despicable people. And people who were never poor.

Am I being unfair? Maybe I am. How can I . . .? Some of my moments are muddled. Moments of a fury that I hold against the entire world, I who walk here along a barren road of babassu palms and shacks. Is it perhaps just not possible to divide people into the lucky and the unlucky?

But, if I see that some people are so much happier than others . . . that there are people who turn into animals because there are no parties . . . There are no parties . . . If there are little girls suffering facelessly through picnics in Manjopi . . . There are children turning into animals, how can I not? Is it fair?

I don't know how to understand. How some lucky people swallow gulps of Coca-Cola and then belch and then smile and still don't even know that there are some unlucky faces that can't find parties, and can't stand anything.

I'm leaving. I'll say goodbye to the city of parties, of banquets, of dainties. I lost my taste for all that sweet stuff. I am almost bitter. Because I don't know if I understand how fortune's victims and fortune's darlings pass me by and pass by each other. Unhappy people and happy people.

17

I am poor in father and mother. Poor, poor.

Is that fair? I ask myself if it's fair to ask if it's fair. The sense of fairness is already lost in that unfair way of asking. Is it fair? What can be considered fair? I ask myself as I walk on the bridge and see the beggars. Is it fair? And what can be considered fair? I walk on the bridge and there are beggars lining my path. And robbers and prostitutes. So I don't identify with them. And yet I do. I stare at them but I don't find myself in the pupil of their eyes. And yet I do. They don't reflect, they are not a clear and limpid mirror. I see myself. What are they? They must be something, since they reflect something. But what? That's what's not fair. That's the unfair thing. That's what makes me weep with guilt over the rolls in the snack on the Varig plane. And I'm the one who feels guilty because I am already conscious of it. They are guilty but unconscious. But they don't escape from being guilty too. Is that it? What else could it be? What could it be that doesn't allow me to walk on the bridge without bursting into questions? I only want to cross the bridge to get to the other side, what nonsense. I only want to get to the other side. What a load of rubbish.

I'm traveling a road thousands of miles long to Tijucopapo. I'm not going to get stuck by a bridge. I'm going to cross it. I left my home and the city because I lost the beginning, the birth of my mother who was the lady of the house where on Sundays nobody used to speak to each other. I'm going to Tijucopapo crossing bridges where I'm discovering that maybe it isn't possible to divide up into fair and unfair, into rich and poor. Where I'm falling into a relativity so great that it seems I'm lacking the will to carry on. Will there be nothing left that can be affirmed? Everything seems to be so relative that it would be better to stop right here on top of a stone.

Damn it.

Damn it. In 1969, at Christmas, we retreated from the wonderful beaches of Boa Viagem. The Boa Viagem of Recife – of the city-between-rivers, fiery and flooded. Of Recife the pitiful. We beat a dawn retreat in the midst of pigs and chickens and bits of tapioca, among the shaking and the shuddering of a migrant truck, to a filthy hotel in Bras in São Paulo while papa, the loonie, rented some basement or other to stuff us into. And this is not just another story. This is not at all the fucking shit of just another story. I repeat: we withdrew from the still-beautiful beaches of Boa Viagem for rotten old Bras in São Paulo. And I'll repeat that it was a matter of leaving behind the landscape of the sea and unloading our traveling eyes in the depths of a hotel in Bras where a man is masturbating into a washtub. So that was the first thing: a guy rubbing his dick against the tub in the courtyard of the hotel. I had already seen plenty of sex at the back of the backyards. After that came the card marked with the price of apples on a barrow on the streets of Bras. Not the apple itself. The apple from São Paulo that they said could only be equaled in heaven. The apple I wouldn't ever get to taste. In Recife there were no apples for poor people. Only in the choices of apple-or-pear that we played. Apple or pear? Nema . . . Recife, where the fruits are hard. Recife, and its macaíbas and its pitombas. But São Paulo would never be the paradise in the pamphlets they used to distribute about it back there in poor old Recife.

Peyote, Nema. To get away from all these things. I should have smoked some but never did. I can't believe I was so stupid. I spent half of my adolescence reading the 91st Psalm.

Damn it.

I left home because I didn't have the courage to smoke peyote in order to get away from there. I left home because, when I got home at night, my brothers and sisters hadn't left me any food. My brothers and sisters, the vandals. That's exactly how I used to refer to them in my moments of rage. I left home because the food was bought with my money and my brothers and sisters didn't leave me any supper. I left home for various reasons. Because people used to either quarrel with each other or else not speak to one another. Because they were spiteful, because . . .

18

I'm in bad shape today. I'm really not well today. I walked a very short way today. I spent the morning in the shack where I slept, the house of an old couple. I ate there, stayed there drowsing in the oldness of the old folk, thought for hours along the lines of how I'd even give up my young body so as not to have to go on, so as to be able to go back, so as to at least be able to see Jonas's face again and beg him on the telephone:

"I love you, please come back."

Never mind my pride, my dignity, never mind that my body might melt into tears at his feet:

"I love you . . ., please."

Then, when the sun shone midday and made shadows behind our backs I sent everything to hell and stood up to carry on – I needed to persevere. But I only walked for two hours. Here I am again sitting on a stone, with Jonas's shadow following me. How can a man . . .

How can a man desert me? How can a man stop loving? I can't believe it. If I had a telephone right now I'd call Jonas:

"Jonas? Yes, it's me. It's Risia, the one who loves you. Jonas, I'm on the brink of death because of you. You know that, don't you? So, why? Why?"

Oh, if I could only kill myself. If I could kill myself I would kill myself.

But my anger makes me persevere. I don't deserve the pain that Jonas caused me. Jonas doesn't deserve to have me weep over him.

"Jonas, go fuck yourself."

I want to get to Recife straight away. When I get close to Recife, I'll take a side road that takes me to the beaches of Boa Viagem and run till I meet the waves. I'll swallow some salt and swim miles out until I'm exhausted. So my exhausted body will sleep and forget Jonas. So, he didn't die then?

"You should have died once and for all, damn you."

Damn it.

The things I say no longer make any sense. God, where am I going to end up?

I would like to live in the hiding place of the Most High and abide under the shadow of the Almighty and say to the Lord that He is my refuge and my fortress – in Whom I put my trust. I'd ask him to deliver me from the fowler's snare and from deadly pestilence; and to cover me with his feathers, so that I should be safe under his wings, and his truth would be my shield and my buckler. And with Him I shall not fear the terrors of the night, nor the arrow that flies by day, nor the pestilence that stalks through the darkness, nor the slaughter that strikes at midday.

Midday is my worst time.
The church bells toll ninety-one psalm strokes.
In the street they throw stones at me:
"There goes Miss Holy-Moley. The walking hymnbook."
I spit on them.
They don't know me. They never knew me.
Just because I defend certain principles, they suppose . . .

They don't understand that I'm a person debating with myself here over the feeling of disillusion that comes from discovering the relativity of the world. The 91st Psalm is totally stupid. Unfortunately. The only thing that serves to transport to the Realms on High is peyote.

But I didn't use peyote. And today neither peyote nor the 91st Psalm nor any other shit will help me believe, help me fall under some illusion. Nothing will, unless it's a landscape I'm coloring with crayons on a white sheet of paper. My box of twenty-four colored crayons. My illusion. My waxy revolution.

And the bastards still throw stones at me in the street. Even though they don't know me.

Up to a certain age I never used to go to sleep without asking

God to protect me from bogeymen, from ghosts, from burglars and other things that do evil in the night. I was terribly fearful. So I would pray. And so I would repeat the 91st Psalm.

Now it doesn't work any longer. Not because I've lost my fears. I haven't. Quite the contrary – the 91st Psalm increased my fears so much that it got to the point of making itself completely useless. It sometimes seems to me that God is a monster, the product of a magic mixture from some witch's boiling cauldron, created just to scare us stiff.

I don't know if God exists. I tend to think he probably doesn't. I'd rather believe in ghosts and witches.

19

Today I woke up with an immense loathing for the world. My whole stomach was churning and I couldn't eat the breakfast they offered me in the shack. I'm thinking about how many shacks I've passed through so far. How many cities and wretched villages. I don't know exactly. But I feel that every day I'm penetrating further into the forest. I'm just continuing parallel to the road. I don't want to see the cars traveling on the highway, the cars that are certainly coming from São Paulo or going to São Paulo. I left home. Today I've been invaded by a loathing for the world. There's an inherent disposition towards vomiting in me; that's what's showing up today and every stench makes me feel worse. I can't stand the smell of anything. I can't stand the presence of any animal in the branches of the trees or crossing in front of me. Today all the animals are possums. Dung. The stenches of the world. The highways that take cars to São Paulo from where I left home one day when my father decided to rummage in my closet. Yesterday I spent a night of many dreams but among them was one which was that I really am traveling to Tijucopapo however much it costs me. I'm traveling to Tijucopapo and I know that behind me remains the man I loved and love. How should I talk about him now? Like so: The man I love remains behind me. How should I talk about him now? Yesterday I spent a night of many dreams among which was one about a man's penis. I dreamed last night about a man's penis, a warm excitable member I always touched like someone touching wonders that grow in one's hands and that wet themselves like a child. Among my dreams . . . Today is a morning of reverberating sun and I walk on agonized by his presence that comes to me in dreams of the most different shades of color and then abandons me alone on the road I'm traveling. But I'm going to Tijucopapo. Even though I'll be a lost soul there. Even though there I'll be a soul lost to whatever beauty might be found in shamelessness. Yes, I'm going, because there I'll lose myself and lose. Yes, because there's always a beautiful side to shamelessness. In a man who betrays his wife with another, in the woman who betrays her husband with another, there exists a beautiful and romantic impossibility which always reminds me of Romeo and Juliet, which turns love into another feeling, maybe even more rich, maybe even more intense, and even, maybe, more beautiful. And so sincere that in the end it doesn't seem to be a betrayal at all; so that the word betrayal was created by me, and so that maybe everything is really loving, loving in every tone of sound, in every shade of color. I myself am the first to discover the glory in men's round crowned member. A man's penis is glorious. I am the first one for whom a man's penis was many times enclosed in her mouth. I close my mouth. But I can't disrespect the little girl inside of me. Who's seated on a throne, and that's why I'm going to Tijucopapo. Even though I may be a lost soul there for whatever beauty there is in shamelessness. Even though I lose the thousands of parties and the thousands of lights in wealthy São Paulo. Even though I have to forgo my pleasure in the brilliance of the lights, in the variety of flavors. Forgo the liquors in the thousands of bars. Forgo the lines at the cinema and forgo the dinners in the restaurants. Even though I'm not the blond woman with the dark glasses in the smart car. Even though I . . . No, I didn't sleep around with any other man when I lost the man I loved. No, I wouldn't sleep around with another man, not even if I knew that what I was losing out on might be love, in all its many aspects. Only because I can't stand that. I can't stand the way it's done in São Paulo. In São Paulo you lose the love of a man and you are exposed to everything. São Paulo is a game that I can't play. And it really breaks my heart to have to accept that São Paulo has its own way of doing things. I wanted to be able to shout out: "stupid raving crazy spook city! I want to get out!" In São Paulo you lose the love of a man and you are exposed to everything. Or even when you have the love of a man. In Tijucopapo, with the man I'll meet, it seems less dangerous. But what about if that's not true? Or is it cowardly? No. It's a question of establishing limits and that's that. That expression "and that's that" is my limit. We live in the immensity of the universe, and above us is infinity, very far away according to mama. The word shamelessness was invented by mama. But I'm giving in and confessing that I'll need to enclose myself inside a house and white walls so as not to fly from house to house like a fine thread or the feather of a bird. Since only a bird flies like only a bird can. What hurts me in shamelessnesses, or why I suffer when I come across them, is because I come from a world already so shameless through my father and mother, through Lita, through my aunt . . . What I want to do is mend my world. It was because of discovering and fighting very early on against people's shamelessness that I lost all confidence in people's dignity. Even though I knew very well that shamelessness might well not exist if I put on spectacles and discerned that shamelessness is the same as weakness. And discerned that there are people who had perfect worlds with a father and mother and who, for that very reason, long for imperfection. At that point everything appears harmonious and I shut up and have nothing more to say. Up till the moment of my suffering. I shut up till the moment of my suffering. Because someone is responsible for it. Because it is why I cry out loud. Because I cannot disrespect the child that exists inside me. That is seated on a throne. Because the cause of my shattering into pieces lies in the shamelessness committed by people. And I do not forgive for my suffering. Even if I have to put up with swallowing the fact that shamelessness is nothing more than slackness and weakness. Or that shamelessness is the strength that I don't have. And that, therefore, shamelessness is a thing that doesn't exist.

20

The word *thing* is the proper undefinition of everything.

The people of São Paulo no longer know how to talk. They chatter on saying that everything is a thing, calling everything some sort of thing. I have a longing for the pretty names I'll find again in Tijucopapo. In Tijucopapo I pick jambos every afternoon with an earthenware basin. There are fearsome cavies in the furrows. There are the flour shed, the mill, the lush fields of cane. In São Paulo I could only find words in a foreign language, or in an awful dumbness. In São Paulo I almost lost my speech.

Once, in São Paulo, I bought a camera to take photographs of my mother and my brothers and sisters but I ended up heading for the zoo to take photographs of the animals because my brothers and sisters were vandals and had quarreled with each other at that time, and had quarreled with my mother as well. And I had quarrelled with them too, obviously. So there was a horrible resentful atmosphere at home and I went to the zoo to photograph the animals.

I left São Paulo because when I was there I wanted everything to come to a halt in me, but I had arrived too late and everything was already set up in high-rises, in building sites, in avenues. I wanted everything to come to a halt in me, I wanted not to be contradicted, I wanted to be like the Bible, the greatest book, the 91st Psalm, God's commands. I wanted to be God so I could kill all the people I wanted to, and make the world in my own way. Truthfully, in São Paulo my dream was always to be a diplomat, an ambassadress, some important political figure or other. The president of a country. A presidency would surely be the highest pinnacle, me in command, me in the cabinet, me in the center, me in power – I would be the greatest dictator in the history of all time. I think I would kill off half the world, I'd wage war on anyone who chanced across my warpath, I'd go crazy once and for all. I'd want everything to come to a halt in me because I couldn't stand knowing that there were a thousand exits, countless entrances. It was always so painful to pass through so many entrances and so many exits, it was labyrinthine, I used to get lost, I used to cry. São Paulo is very big, it has buldings with thousands of stories invading the sky, it has infinite avenues, I can easily get lost there, I am exposed to all dangers. In order not to suffer I needed to have control of the world: so that neither this nor that would ever happen because I couldn't stand it; so that these, those, and the others would be eliminated because they did thus and such that hurt me; so that certain acts like this one or that one wouldn't happen again because they touched me to the quick (and I am a quickened woman); so: off with Tom's head, beat up on Dick, kill . . . My orders.

I understand all the presidents in the world.

My code of laws and directives would be something crazy. But maybe not. It might happen, I think it just might, it might happen that I sit in the armchair where the president should sit and start crying just from the mere sight of a long table of ministers staring at me. If I were president, I'd cry.

And, anyway, my ideas are quite absurd. My desires are quite absurd. And, anyway, I'm so far away from everything now. Nobody knows that I am wandering in the immensity of a forest. Did I separate myself off too much, perhaps? When I die I ought to put a notice in the newspaper so that people would know. I want them to know. A forest is immense. Nevertheless, I would still like to control the world. How does one control a forest? How does one drain a river? How does one cleave an avenue?

An engineer knows how. Yes, if I'd studied engineering my life might have been better. An engineer must know the processes of the world and have more power.

Yes, I should have studied engineering. An engineer doesn't have any real problems with questions, does he? An engineer does things and that's that. That's that. Way over there, then down below, passes the deep, black, and powerful highway that takes cars to São Paulo and brings them back from São Paulo. In a toing-and-froing that does go somewhere, finally. The highway. Engineers construct something that's capable of taking things somewhere. The answers lie in science. I'm not at all scientific. And that's why I cry so much. My children will be engineers. I shall compel them to be engineers. I don't care. I'll compel them. So they won't be snivelers. So they won't be fairies or pansies. Nowadays, the man who isn't an engineer is a pansy. I'll compel my children.

Sometimes, when I finish off a thought like that, I think I'd be a terrible mother. Could it be that I'll be a terrible mother? I don't think so. Maybe not, because at the moment of shouting at my son: "You shall be an engineer, do you hear?" I'll cry and beg him to forgive me because I'm a bit crazy. And I'll own up to the mud I'm made of. And I'll tell him about Tijucopapo. And I'll contradict everything. I'll say that my way of conceiving things can't exist; nobody *is* an engineer. A person studies engineering. Nobody *is* anything. The most there can be is that somebody studied something. One cannot be any thing. The verb *to be* is . . .

It seems strange to say that the verb *to be* is a thing. The verb *to be* is something or other, some essence that doesn't go with the word *engineer.* I don't know. And it's always somehow in such thoughts about being that I get all tangled up and have to stop because I lost the thread. I only know that I would tearfully tell my child that I am a liar. And that, as far as fairies and pansies and my own morality are concerned, I almost had an affair with a woman.

I almost had an affair with a woman and I'm leaving the city because I can't stand the city. The city exposes me to the most dangerous dangers, and crimes, and outrages. I very much regret knowing that I'm going to lose all the parties, because deep down I'm fascinated by lights and glitter. But it so happens that at parties there aren't only lights and glitter. At parties there are sweet sufferings that break hearts like mine.

21

I am leaving the city where I became a woman but where I arrived a child. It appears that the one survived at the cost of the other and therefore I needed to come away. Now I'd like to compose an aria which will recompose my journey along the road. I want to compose an aria which will send out music as fine as the strings of a violin. An aria-history of my journey from the road through this forest. Of my travels through the forest. An aria that will be the letter I'll write when I get to Tijucopapo, the land where my mother was born. An aria that covers from my departure to my arrival. I want to compose an aria which will recompose my retreat along the road and from the road to the fields, these fields, where I hope to find the flowers I'll paint with wax crayons on my landscape, in the letter to my mother. I want to compose an aria to recompose my rage and turn it into a gentle beloved little girl. I want to compose an aria of love to echo in the caves of this mountain I am on.

I am at the foot of this mountain. We humans are much smaller than mountains. There's no doubt about that. The mountains here on my journey are monstrous black rocks. There are shacks at their feet, I am at their feet. And I am a human who is nothing. A mountain is full of imposing chasms that threaten what I am – the fragile body of a human being smaller than a mountain. A human being is smaller than a mountain. There's no doubt about that. Being at the foot of a mountain extinguishes all the possibilities I might have of thinking about myself, of recognizing myself and knowing how to go on. I don't know if I know how to go on. I'm coming through the green valleys of farms belonging to others until what I see are flowers.

I came through the green valleys of the farms of others until what I see are flowers. This should be the twentieth day. "The twentieth day": could that be in the Bible? I wish it were. So as to give what happened to me the tone of fulfilling a punishment from God. Or of a mission from God that I were in the midst of accomplishing, on the way to Jerusalem. I stopped for twenty days at the foot of this mountain. I made a bonfire and protected myself from the sun and the rain in the mouth of a cave. It must be the twentieth day. I forgot to mark it down on a tree trunk like

73

Robinson Crusoe. My watch broke as soon as I left São Paulo, and I'm not in São Paulo noting the days by my packet of pills. I won't take any more pills. In São Paulo, the first sign of being without a man, of being inside the solitude of a love that's over, is to stop taking the pill. I won't take any pills in Tijucopapo. Or could this be the twenty-eighth day? I ate some bread and dried meat that I'm carrying in a bag. I ate the fruits I found and drank water from a stream that runs down below. *Robinson Crusoe* was the first great book I read. But the best stories were those my father told me, the idiot. My father told me stories like no one else has ever since. I stopped here about twenty days and composed an aria recomposing the stories my father told me.

First Movement: – My father is a son of a bitch.

Second Movement: – My father is a son of a bitch.

Third Movement: – My father is a son of a bitch.

When I was ready to leave home, I left once and for all on this road that became my own. That became my home. At least it became my home, since my life would be always linked to theirs, when I was on the point of leaving home and was only waiting to explode.

I exploded on the day that papa messed around in my closet.

ME: Papa! You've been messing around in my closet.

HIM: Yes, I did. Who do you think you are in this house to dare . . .

ME: Papa! (*A hysterical cry.*) Papa, you'd better get it clear that here I'm the one who has a salary as high as yours. That I am who I want to be. That you haven't existed since I was five years old. That if you want to exist as an authority figure, you'd better know you're a pure shit. I'm no longer a minor and it's time for you to understand that your place is in hell.

Don't you dare mess around in my closet, ever again, do you hear me? Or I'll kill you. Papa, I'm still prepared to kill you!

Papa gave me a couple of clouts around my brainpan and I fell down in a sort of a faint. When I came to there were the traces of tears in my eyes, a sadness taking full shape. I would have to leave. I would not permit them to beat up on me, a woman. That was several months ago. I wouldn't really kill my father. My father is a great man, the motherfucker. He used to tell stories like no one else ever did. I'm still on the byways of this road that takes me to my home, but my life will be forever linked to theirs. The other night I stayed in the hut of some Xavante people who reminded me the whole time of them, of papa, mama, and the children. It was a large family with a bunch of little kids, stunted and pot-bellied with kilos of worms in their guts. There were about a dozen of them. The shack was filled with the dregs of humanity from door to door. They were really, really poor and the children formed a line of "efs": Francisco, Francisxio, Francisca, Francisval, Fransérgio, Fátima, Fábio, Fransilvia, Fransonia, and so on, and so on.

I left home because my wages were the highest and even so my brothers and sisters didn't leave any food for me, and even so the son of a bitch of my father still dared to mess around in my closet and committed the crime of raising his hand to the face that never faced up to him, to my face. I'm going to Tijucopapo to find out why my father used to enjoy hitting me so much.

My wages were the highest in the house, and my mother lodged all her hopes in my person. I couldn't stand to be suffocated like that and left to come here. I left home because on Sunday days people would glance at each other trying to guess what it was that they didn't want to say out loud. Since I couldn't stand that, and since I am so intelligent that lost women appear to me searching for my advice on the pain of loving a lover, since I am so intelligent and vomit with great facility when faced with a house like that on days of Sunday, and days of a city like São Paulo, a city of lost women, I got out. I got out and I want to compose an aria which recomposes my retreat in retrospective.

My father is the reminder of all my mortification. He came to me slowly, over twenty days, but I didn't want him to come. Since I couldn't care less. I couldn't care less about my father anymore and I don't even know where he lives. I am loosed onto life. It became time to come and I came. It became time to begin living, I set out on the road, with trembling lips. I left home because papa's presence mortified my life. Papa was just like a spook. I also couldn't put up with the sickening intimacy of my brothers and sisters any longer: they'd come home late at night buzzing around the room where I was trying to sleep and struggling with me to share fleas. My brothers and sisters only didn't totally gang up on me because . . . I only know that they nearly ganged up on me. I had the highest wages. And that was horrible because I was getting to hate them. I come from a very poor family and I'm going to spend my life trying to find out the reason for this unfairness. It's really horrible to be poor. You begin to hate your brothers and sisters because they don't leave any food for you and because you sleep in the same room where they come home to sleep and buzz around. I come from a very poor family. When we had been in São Paulo for two years, papa was arrested for smuggling. Papa is a hero, too. It's really horrible to be poor – you want to kill your father, you don't love your mother. Your dream is to be a lawyer, a diplomat, a politician, and you can't be because your father sullied the family name even more by getting himself jailed for smuggling. So you spend the rest of your

76

life dreaming about being the dictator mistress of the world that you couldn't conquer with your papa and mama.

When I was about to leave home, mama asked me:

"What's going on?"

I said:

"It's the Revolution! The Revolution!"

22

I left because it wasn't working out. I couldn't reconcile myself to unhappiness. To a life that always conveyed some sort of anguish. I would sometimes resort to politics to try to explain it. As I resorted to religion, as I resorted to the devil's own worth of philosophies and psychologies. I would sometimes think about politics: We're a gang of animals led by a gang of animals. We are animals. Nothing remains to be done. We are animals – tele-controlled, managed, massified, spied upon, observed, framed, boxed up together inside the prison of the street. A bunch of animals. A herd of tame animals. I spit. We are animals. I expectorate. We are animals. I vomit. We are animals. I turn two cartwheels one after the other in the broad field I'm walking through. We—are—an—i—mals. I trace pirouettes in the air. We—are—an—i—mals. I turn somersaults. We—are—an—i—mals. And I fall down tired sprawling over the ground. Shattering into pieces. Hurting myself. Silly, mindless, labyrinthine. And I cry. No we're not. No—we're—not. And I sob. No—we're—not. No—we're—not. And I sit on a boulder and cry for hours and hours so's I don't have to admit that we are animals. If I believed that we are the animals we are, and that we will therefore carry on caged in, chained up, chained together, slaves for ever (for-ever?) and that there remains nothing to be done, . . . If I thought that nothing remained for me to do, I'd go mad. And madness is the margin I can't stand. Not the margin. I prefer the middle of the crowd, the mass, the components in the current that leads us to nothingness but that leads us there together. Not the margin. Not the solitude of a madman. I get up abruptly from the stone, dry my face, and burrow into the middle of the forest where the animals love each other. It's there, in the middle of the forest, that love is found. We are not wild animals. We are silly sheep looking for love. And, there's nothing else that I want. I want the love of a family on Sundays. I've found out that it's with love that you feel good. I think I'm traveling in order to get married. In the middle of the forest coatis caress each other, monkeys open their mouths and kiss other monkeys on the mouth, female panthers roar as they are penetrated by voracious males. Hisses, roars, whistles, shrieks, rutting, spittle and blood, tearing and tunneling and kissing and cuddling. Foliage, waterfalls, and love, love.

I alone reach this love. Every road leads there – to love.

What an outrage that there should be a man who died for me. What hatred.

I left São Paulo because there was a man who died for me and because there I lived in the suburbs whereas all my friends were well established in São Paulo's Higienópolis. And then it was often impossible to keep in touch because I didn't have a telephone. I was never told about anyone's death, for example. Keeping in touch was difficult. São Paulo's Higienópolis is where people drink whole Guaranás. It's where the people are who've already read the books I read. And that's what hurts me. It's knowing that it isn't Nema who's going to read the books I'll read – Nema doesn't speak English – it isn't Ilsa, the housemaid, it's not even my mother, and it's far less likely to be the beggar on the bridge. I got tired of spending my money on taxis going to and coming from parties in São Paulo's Higienópolis.

When I get there, I'll tell Nema about the thousand scientific and nonscientific names they concocted to define me and to prove their innocence in my departure. When they want to, they invent whatever names they want to, but the one word they can actually articulate is *thing*. That is, everything and nothing. But we have to meet at whatever the place is where there is only one truth. Since I don't believe that we are here for no reason and that afterwards everything is over. I don't believe it. My theory on death is that . . .

Oh, . . . I . . . when I die I'm going to have to stick a notice in the newspaper, so that people know about it, at least. That's the way, because I am now so far away from people, I separated myself so much from them that they no longer hear anything about me. I no longer have an address, I no longer have a place to stay. And also because, in one way or another, people are going to want to know if I died or not. They're going to want to know when I died. They are going to see something or other when I die. It seems as though I know a lot about my death. It seems as though I know a lot less about my life. That's really something. Not knowing is some thing.

Nema, do you think that in São Paulo there exists a poem in which emu rhymes with Nema? No, there everything is dissonance.

23

My father is the reminder of all my mortification. We were such a poor family that I ended up not being able to bear it any more on Sundays. I was already a completely shattered little girl. I couldn't even watch television from so much oppression by papa and mama. They were such shits. I couldn't even play. When the television arrived in my street I was already a completely enraged little girl. I had already been out begging. I could almost cry about it. I asked for charity with a tin can in my hand: "A little rice; a piece of bread, for the love of God."

I'm leaving now to paint the revolution in wax colors.

What I'm doing is thinking. The women of Tijucopapo must be like me, making a shadow on the ground. I am a woman of Tijucopapo. I'm leaving now. I'm leaving now because of those movies, movies, movies . . . moving pictures playing in front of me on the weekends in São Paulo. And at night I would have nightmares. Those movies, pictures playing on the weekend right before our eyes. It's a danger. I think it's dangerous. I knew people who traveled to places where English was spoken simply because in the movies English was spoken, and it seemed like another life, it seemed as if it would be better and more beautiful. But it was all an illusion. So off they went, in search of a life that didn't exist. Dangerous. Because they never ever got there. They never made it. And they came back with no life at all. They had lost their life here too. And they came back without the life from there, the life they hadn't found. Those pictures rolling huge colored balls before us, those weekend movies are dangerous mechanical illusions.

My box of colored pencils is harmless.

I'm leaving to paint the revolution, today, the twentieth day. I'm under orders from Christ.

It's so difficult.

It's very difficult.

It's difficult even believing that I'll be able to go right to the end. Few people have. And that makes everything harder. Moreover, the few people who went didn't leave any tracks, a ready-made path. But no ready-made path would also serve me. I have to slash open my own way through the forest, I have to do it myself. No other path would serve me. And that makes everything harder. The sun melts down on my head, my skin gets darker and darker, I'll arrive in Tijucopapo black, sweating like a black. I'm thirsty, too. When I get near Recife, I'll take a side road that takes me to the center, to the São José market, I'll stop at a stand and drink iced sugarcane. I'll drink iced sugarcane in the tumult of the São José market, the machine pressing the cane into husks before my eyes swiveling among the thousands of scenes and stories of that market that's crazy with people, with mud, with root plants, with the smells of all the vegetables, with the colors of all the vegetables, with the sounds of all the vendors' cries and all the varied music.

I'll spend some time in the filth of that São José market and I don't know why.

But I'm going to. And I'll ask all the angels. I'll call up a choir of angels to help me on my journey. I'll ask them to play their trumpets in heaven until the sounds scatter echoes on Earth and the voices of a thousand angels protect me from the temptation of evil. Until I was a certain age I knew the 91st Psalm by heart. If I still knew it, I probably wouldn't hesitate to recite it in the middle of these nights ahowled by packs of starving wolves, sung by swollen frogs, by little crickets, by snakes lying in ambush, in the middle of these menacing nights where I lie down to sleep and glimpse stars through the openings in the shacks I'm stopping at, almost dead from the death of him who died and left me exposed to all dangers. If only I could pray. I am too scientific to believe in what I pray for. If only I could believe. If only I could telephone. If only I could hear, coming from the heavens, the voices of a choir of angels: the 91st Psalm.

24

If I find a peyote bush along the road I'll cut off a leaf and make myself some tea.

The morning landscape you see from an airplane, with the sun on high, is the vision of paradise, a hallucination. Suddenly, you are high above the clouds in the blue sky, and below lies paradise made of white feathers. The next time I'll ask them to open the window so I can touch God. It's cowardly not to let us open the window of the plane.

So heaven is close by, mama.

"Do you think that heaven is that close?" mama used to ask when I wanted very much to have something that she couldn't give me. When I ardently desired to have socks with pompons on for Christmas. I waited for those socks the whole year long. Telling mama that I'd like socks with pompons on and she repeating that heaven wasn't so close. When Christmas came, Santa Claus didn't bring me my socks and mama shouted from the kitchen at me sniveling in the living room with no pomponed socks in my hands: "Do you think heaven is that close?" Heaven. Damn it, damn it, mama. You are crazy. So it's heaven you put as your limit? Heaven . . . it's clear that heaven was going to be a long way off ahead of the little girl I used to be. But, listen, heaven doesn't exist and that's that. Heaven is where the Varig planes go as they convey me around. Only heaven knows how to be ironically blue up there above me while down here below I die my death of ashy gray rain from not having got socks with pompons on for Christmas because heaven was far away, an unattainable limit. I can touch heaven, mama, in the clouds through the plane window.

When I get there, I'm certain to have seen flowers, I want to see red flowers, when I get there, after I've passed through beds ot red flowers in the middle of the fields, I'm going to translate this letter into English and send it.

I'm going to tell mama everything I thought.

I already cried like never before, because it was so horrible to be poor.

I am traveling to paint the revolution that won't knock my one and only whole Guaraná down from the counter. I want it to be Christmas night when I get there. I want to appear on the television and on the movie screens.

I think a lot so as to see if from one comparison to another I can understand things better. But, among other things, I lie. I got to the point of lying. I almost lost my speech around certain things. I'll send a letter. Meanwhile, there are some stories of mine that I'm ashamed of, and I'll lie about them.

I'm going back to Tijucopapo to see if I know. It was there that my mother was born. I had to leave. I'm going there to see if I know why I'm able to be cruel and not love as well as hate. I'm going to Tijucopapo to see if I know why I am poor. Afterwards, I'll paint the revolution.

On my road there are babassu palm trees and shacks. I don't quite know why I'm traveling out here, maybe because I am so cruel. I want to see flowers.

What frightens me is that some people are so much happier than others . . . I, for example, could never be the drum majorette that I always died of desire to be in the parades on Independence Day. Brother Jorge and Sister Naninha, Nema's parents, were so happy there in their life alone together, and so much in agreement about everything, and in their belief in the same God, and so on. Mama and papa were sheer hell. Papa betrayed mama with Analices, mama was pitiful, given away, pregnant, stagnant, apathetic. Papa was an atheist, mama was a believer. From them only unhappiness and death could come. Or it was just

83

me, the idiot. I'm going to see if I know why I think I'm an idiot. We were very poor. I'm going to see if I know why there are girls who can be drum majorettes in the parades on Independence Day, while I never could.

If I could only growl . . . Oh, if I could be an animal I'd be a mare, a mare that would take off like a shot kicking up clods of mud in the sodden fields or raising dust clouds out of the dry earth in the mountains. And that's how I would forget, God, that I lost the love of a man. I'd forget how one day I sat at a table in a bar and hurt a man. Although I didn't want to hurt him. But he got hurt and died. And I traveled five hundred thousand miles trying to be the mare that up till today I'm still trying to be and haven't been able to. Today I am, among other things, a woman who tried to be a mare and didn't manage it. I'll turn ten cartwheels in the field to see if I turn into a mare.

I know I am a person assailed by tormenting memories. I tremble. And I'm afraid. My stomach is churning all over.

People decided to trust in me when they would lose all trust in themselves. They decided to leave, subtly, to my account what didn't fit into theirs.

I was such a little girl.

There are still days when I wake up stammering.

25

I left São Paulo because there, whatever I wanted to do I couldn't. Because there there was no rain, no sand, no pitomba. There, whatever I wanted I couldn't do. There, sometimes, there in those streets as evening fell, there I'd stop on the median in the middle of the street waiting for the cars to pass, indifferent and forlorn, and trying to tell myself I was a whore: "I'm a whore, take me anywhere you want to." Because that was the only way I could surrender myself to the complete and total indifference that comes from giving my own body, without pride, without dignity, without love, without pain.

I left São Paulo so as not to be a whore. Because we were very poor. And I had lost the love of Jonas.

Getting there is really tiring. How many thousands of miles away must I be? Two hundred and fifty? Are there any more to go still? On my road are babassu palms and shacks. I'm a woman traveling alone on the highway.

Sometimes I stop on a bridge, by a boulder, I sit down on the edge and strum a bit of music on the guitar I'm carrying, or apply a few different colors with my wax crayons on a landscape.

Sometimes I need to stop.

The fact is that here I am, a woman traveling alone on the highway. My beginning remained way back there behind a whole range of mountain ranges.

Avoiding it doesn't get me anywhere. The landscape of a journey is trees and stones and an occasional shack and cows grazing. Some vegetable vendor or another crosses my path early in the morning. He goes by bareback on a sluggish donkey heading for the city. The landscape of a journey is winds and the sun of many days of walking and the moon of the nights between the growls and whistles of all the animals.

Everything happened precisely in the time of a little girl. The rest, life, is redundant.

I'll never disrespect the little girl that exists inside me. The little girl that exists inside me is seated on a throne. The world is not in so much agreement over relativity as I sometimes think. But I can transform the world with wax crayons. I'm going to paint a revolution.

In the center of São Paulo city there was reinforced concrete structured against me. Reinforced over my head, just as a mango tree in Lita's yard structured itself in my shadow. That was the impression that collapsed on top of me from those overhead highways as I walked below on an island surrounded by cars on all sides, walking like a prostitute.

Today I ate a pineapple. It's been a long time. Today it's the evening and the sky is the blue of almost seven o'clock at night. It's extraordinary that it's not Recife here. In Recife night took a long time to fall. But when it was winter, and as night closed in each evening, in Recife the rain would fall, like a waterspout. It would rain and the saturated rooftops slithered wetly. The rain rained down from the saddest of skies. I would watch it beat down through the window. I dreamed about Recife yesterday, about those waterlogged fields that could be seen from the house I lived in. That city doesn't fade in my memory, it comes to me in dreams.

But I loved Recife.

In São Paulo, later, came the autumn. Later autumn would come and I'd know that I lied many times. I lied frequently. At times I lied a lot. That was something else. But my lies are states of dreaming. Dreaming I always dreamed.

If I had smoked some dope, I would have dreamed even more. In São Paulo I didn't smoke dope myself, but my friends used to smoke it and I inhaled all the fumes that hung around near them. I would get intoxicated through them. There was always a bit of smoke left for me after they'd swallowed theirs down. And I learned that I love my friends. And it's that very intoxication I know I need. It was that very intoxication that I had to leave and come away from. But I know that I love. It was with great love that my friends stayed friends even when I couldn't telephone them any more. My friends are what I love best, even though I didn't tell them I had to leave. When I die, I'll have the news published in the paper so they know. What a pity. But I left my best girlfriends and came along the edge of the road. With no little piece of white lace from their hands. Nobody told me, "Good-bye, Risia." Nobody kissed me.

I ran away.
Good-bye, Risia.
And today I can no longer stand this lack of dialogue. This lack of people talk.
I ran away.

Good-bye, Risia.
But now I need my girlfriends' conversation. I almost lost my speech in São Paulo, but the friends I had were like clear water for me to drink from. I'm sick of the absence of conversation. I want someone to say to me, to talk to me:

"Hi, how are you?"
"OK. Do you think I'll be able to make it?"
"Sure, I think you'll make it. You're Risia. From what I know of you, you'll make it. You know, Risia, things are difficult for me, too. And they are for everyone. But, from what I know about you, you're one of the ones who'll make it, for sure."

"Hi, how are you?"
"OK. Do you think I'll make it, if what's driving me is rage? If I left the friends I love? If I don't know whether I love as much as I hate? I left São Paulo because people there used to throw stones at me."
"Risia, I think that being angry is healthy, too. And love and

hate meet each other where the needle's at zero. Where the needle's at zero is where you feel right, and that's where you're going to get to."

"Hi, how are you?"
"OK. But yesterday I had a lousy day. Because yesterday I
dreamed of the man who died for me. What that man did to me
increased an old hatred of mine that comes from mama and
papa . . ."
"Let's sit down at this table and chat. Let's talk. Then you
can go."

"Hi, how are you?"
"I think I'm off . . ."
"Good-bye, Risia. See you soon. Give me a call."

26

Give me a call, Risia.
Good-bye, Risia.
I love you, Risia.
In São Paulo they stoned me, but I had friends like water –
clear and available for me to drink from.
When I get there, I'm going to write about how much I love
my friends. I'll send word to Pedro about how much I remember
his last words. The day before I left, Pedro and I sat at a table and
chatted.
"It's the loneliness," I said.
"My loneliness hurts me, too," he said. "But it also loves. And
sleeps. Eats. Walks. Weeps. Sings. In truth, solitude doesn't exist. Because our thoughts are never alone, there's always a pile of

them milling around out there. If solitude existed, solitude wouldn't talk. But it talks. Solitude talks so loud, it talks through your elbows, through the flowers, through fish, it overflows through our hair, it makes everything wobble on the surface of the water. It's good to be heard. To have a listening point. Is that poetry, or is it not? I need people too. Sometimes I think I'll never talk again, or go out, or go to the movies with people. And when that happens I'm happy. I like you very much."

"I love you, Pedro."

Pedro's words are words that help me leave.

But I could never again telephone my friends. It's months since I had so much as a conversation. When I had to choose my way of being, I opted for the one I knew best, the way of running away. Shall I have forgotten the alphabet? Shall I still know how to make small talk? Will I stammer? I almost lost my speech in São Paulo, but my friends were Pedro, a discussion that I haven't been worthy of for months. I took on this punishment that God charged me with to go into the forest and stay clear of the BR Highway engineering that brings and takes cars to and from São Paulo. BR number such and such. BR such and such. Out there, in São Paulo, the world takes place in the gullet, in gulps and eructions. And I haven't the least idea what it's all about.

I'm going to have to dream now. It's getting close to midday and I'm going to have to dream so I can stand not having the voices and words of my friends.

I'm in Pedra Branca now. Leaping onto the rocks in the river at Pedra Branca. The waterfall splashes in front of me, limpid and turbulent as always. I came on horseback to bathe in the river. The horse is over there tied to the tree, long-limbed and placid. From here on this rock I can see the whole of Pedra Branca. The hills are smooth and green, with a few houses scattered sparsely among them. The forest shows its dark-green face where the birds all sing and the frogs croak at night. Pedra Branca. There are breadfruit trees bordering all along the road that leads to the river and it's the cashew season now. The laden cashew trees sway in the wind. There's the hint of a fragrance, a fruitifragrance, floating in the air. From far off comes the wail of wood as the saw cuts through it. There is a trace of a lament in all the sounds of this hidden Pedra Branca. But I came here. And I came to stay. And I came here to stay because I hate the trickeries and the betrayals and the lost life stories in those cities that are not Pedra Branca. Here I'm forgotten and hidden away. Here, from this rock here, I listen to the wailing of the wood coming from the yard at my white house on the green hill, Jonas cutting wood for our son's swing. Here evening can be what it used to be, Sunday can have the sunshine it used to have, I'll gather ripe jambos in an earthenware bowl and water the rosebushes full of roses, the shrubs of dahlias and daisies, the lilies and the jasmine from my garden. I'll always have the garden full of jasmine. The turtles make their slow way to the bog, the dog is big and fierce, there are pigs and chickens, there is a glossy black mare for me to ride. Late every afternoon we go out, my mare and I, for a ride around the outskirts of Pedra Branca, liberated in the rain as it falls and penetrates the earth. And let it rain. I no longer cry. I get back home soaked through, my mare and I, very beautiful and free, the two of us, and waiting for me on the verandah are my son and Jonas: love.

27

I came along here and the road was hard. I ran away many times. I ran away like a mare that doesn't want to be imprisoned in the corral. But I ran away, too, when I took off in my horse shape into the huge countryside that lay before my eyes. My torturous memories pricked my rump as they told me of the need for me to make my own road. And that was how I came along this hard and barren road. I was a woman alone traveling on the road. On my way there were babassu palms and shacks. I was two hundred and fifty thousand miles away and I couldn't stand it any longer. And still I went on tortured by the desire to turn back or to stop. And I stopped a number of times. And I sat on a stone and strummed out a tune on the guitar I carried:

> Children don't do
> What I have done
> I couldn't walk
> I tried to run.

A desire to tell children not to do what I did. I couldn't walk at a normal pace, so I ran off, fleeing from that way of life. So then, don't do it. Or else, let children do what they want to do.

Then I still tried out different colors with my wax crayons on a revolutionary landscape. I was a woman alone traveling on the highway. My meeting with Jonas only took place on the outskirts of Pedra Branca. At the entrance to Primavera. The landscape I brought painted on a blank page turned into a revolutionary one. I came to make the revolution that knocks down not my Guaraná on the counter, but those guilty of all the lovelessness I suffered and of all the poverty in which I lived. I'm going to tell all the wretched workers in the factory that they are unhappy wretches because there are brightly lighted parties taking place in São Paulo. And, if they wanted to, they would drink a whole Guaraná because there in São Paulo life keeps on happening in gulps and gullets and eructions. To the children of the factory workers I'll say no, it's not their parents who are to blame when they get beaten because they eat dirt and shit worms. I know who are. And, to the wives of the factory workers, I'll say that, in case they are betrayed and their husbands beat up on them, it's not really their husbands who are to blame. I know who are. The truth is that, back there in São Paulo, there are made-up women turning up at the parties and wearing dark glasses at the wheel of cars on broad lighted avenues – the mistresses. Pedra Branca. I have the love of Jonas and of a son, and we fight together for a just cause.

28

That's how it goes. Midday went by as clouds go by you when you are in an airplane. When you are in an airplane you pass by paradise.

Dreaming I always dreamed.

And that's just how it is. I want my life to have a finale like a cinema movie in the English language. I want everything to have a happy ending.

My talent for deluding myself is greater than my talent for living. The blame belongs to those movie screens playing before my eyes on weekends in São Paulo. They're dangerous.

When Jonas died for me, for example, I decided to delude myself because I wouldn't stand the situation in my life.

When Jonas died for me, I used to still say that he existed.

"Didn't Jonas come today?" they'd ask at a party.

I'd say that Jonas hadn't been able to come but that he sent his love.

"What a pretty blouse!" someone would exclaim.

I'd say that Jonas gave it to me.

"Do you want to go to the movies?" they'd invite me.

I'd say no, because I had a date with Jonas.

When Jonas went and died on me I lied hundreds of times.

Later on I decided I should burn the clothes I wore on the day it happened. And so I did.

Later I played fifty tunes consecutively on the guitar. Then I drew a landscape and painted it in many colors. Then I made a fleet of a hundred paper boats and launched them onto the rainwater.

It was a rainy day the day Jonas resolved to die on me. I left him standing in the middle of the plain and walked away in tears. I left knowing that each person who deserted me would tear me to pieces for ever. I went about torn to pieces. I went about with the desire to know how long I would go on losing people. How long would I keep on feeling pain. How long everything.

The other day I was checking through my rucksacks at a roadside stand and found a letter from Jonas recriminating with me for my skepticism, my hatred. After I'd finished reading the letter I almost couldn't go any further and almost went running back. I almost threw away the half journey I'd already traveled to turn back and – who knows – to get Jonas back again. I spent hours thinking about whether I should turn back. Until I understood my delusion. My talent for deluding myself is greater than my talent for living. But since I decided that the time had now come to start living, I set myself back on the road again, with trembling lips. And here I am. Very close now. Yesterday I tore up Jonas's letters and threw the pieces into a stream that flowed off into some unknown place. I think that now I would sleep with another man.

But why would I sleep with another man now if I said that I'm running away from São Paulo because there you are exposed to the danger of sleeping with everyman? Why? Maybe it's because the sun here completely melts me. I need to feel once more the glory that is a man.

Would I sleep with another man today because traveling is an adventure?

Life is an adventure. We have to live.

The only place mistakes don't exist is in the Pedra Branca I dream about at midday by Jonas's side.

29

The rest is errors and inconclusions.

Today I would sleep with another man because of that sun that melts everything inside me and leaves me black, I'm like a person who's sunstruck, I feel so giddy, it wouldn't take much to make me stumble and fall. I'm sunstruck and I'm labyrinthine. It's because I'm close to Recife and Recife muddles everything up for me. Recife is always dying from a delirium. From a fever of immeasurable degrees. Recife's delirium definitely doesn't come from peyote. It comes from sunstroke. Recife, the sunstruck. Recife is afire in flames of immeasurable degrees.

"Fire!"

"Die, damn you! Consume yourself, damn you! Total out, damn you!"

"Water!"

"Fire!"

"Water!"

When I came to, I was already in Pernambuco territory. Yesterday, when I came to, I was already in Pernambuco territory because there were immense mango trees in the garden of every farm. And when you get to Pernambuco territory you see mango trees. This was Pernambuco territory. It is Pernambuco territory and Recife must be close, close enough so that I can hear the clamor of the São José market. A deafening clamor. Such a deafening deafening that it was as if it had been multiplied twelve million times and I was arriving in São Paulo with its twelve million inhabitants. But the sun is from Recife because it is melting me.

Recife was on fire, hallucinated under its own sun, suffocating, in the same way that it gets flooded – seduced by the waters of its rivers that succumb to the enchantment of the rain – and it suffocates, and it surrenders. No one can analyze the thermic inconsistencies of a city like Recife. If I get to Recife soon maybe there will be time to resist and not sleep with the first man that comes by today and seduces me. Maybe Boa Viagem beach is nearby and I can run and dive into the waves and swim until my body is exhausted – that's the only way it wouldn't sleep with a man today.

But today my body needs a man. My body was sunstruck and labyrinthinine, my body was intoxicated. I wanted to be seduced. I wasn't at the window, but I wanted to be seduced. So, two vegetable vendors happen to cross my path in the early morning and I talked with one virile young man mounted on a donkey. I don't know if I talked about anything in particular. I only know he seduced me. Today there was a night of rare moonlight irradiated with light because the sun had burned fiercely all day long. The sky was black in color. I was black in color. I mounted behind the man on the donkey's back and we rode for a while. We crossed fields at a slow gallop. The man and I rubbing against each other at every stride. We crossed fields, passed by stableyards, by mills, by stony springs, by farm vegetable gardens and orchards, by beds of flowers, we finally passed by beds of red flowers, so I'd seen red flowers, and I'd heard the song of the crickets and the chirping of the owls, and the howling of the wolves, and roars, and whistles and rutting and spittle and blood, the sounds that composed our music, the sounds that came together in an aria that was ours, of him a man and me a woman traversing a night of rare honeyed moon. The man and I alighted in the mares' stables and went in. The man and I lay down on the hay where the mares lie down. It was on the hay that I loved a man under that rare night of honeyed moonlight. I felt that, with that man, I was sleeping with all the other acts I had slept with before with other men. I had come with all the acts and I felt that this act of mine would be almost perfect. The man touched me as if no part of my body were left untouched, I was entirely the man's, I was totally touched, I was divided into thousands of electric cells, I was being voided and invaded as only the salt water of the sea can sweep through me and invade me and exhaust me. I was being deep-plumbed and saturated. The man pressed me against the walls of the mares' stable and penetrated me with his member, fully aroused and strong and warm, invading me, spraying me with spittle, submerging me and saturating me until I cried out in exhaustion and he cried out in exhaustion and we fell onto the edge of a sea of hay. Even then we didn't fall asleep. I wanted a man with all the acts of the previous men, and with the new acts. I wanted the perfection of an act. The man and I moved together in every act. We still didn't sleep. And when I tried to enwrap the man's member with my hands and he got aroused, and when I wanted to appease it in my mouth and he wet himself like a child wets itself, I cried. I cried with my mouth full of liquid salted with tears, I fondled the man's member that I had sucked and slept like someone who has just emerged from the waves of the sea.

30

So, that's how I loved a man today.

Things happen in an interval of wishes and thoughts. You say to yourself that maybe today you might go to bed with another man and not even a clock hand moves on to tell you that the time already went by and you already loved a man.

When I woke up it was raining in torrents and I heard two tremendous thunderclaps. I shivered slightly. It was raining that rain that accompanied me in my tormented memories of mama crossing to the city in a boat for the birth of dead Ismael and me deludedly building a fleet of a hundred paper ships, the *Santa Maria* and the *Pinta* and the *Nina*, which would carry me through the gutters to any place other than the world in which I saw mama suffer nine months with her belly in the air. I live in the world only because there's no place else to live. Because the world, from São Paulo to Recife and to all the places where they make movies, that same world hurts too much.

When I came to, it was raining torrents and I heard a clamor and a booming of . . . what? It sounded like bombs. Bombs? Could it be the Feast of Saint John? If it were, I'd completely lost all sense of time, since I was still heading toward Christmas. Could it be bombs? Or guns? I turned around abruptly. The man was watching me very calmly lying beside me. He was a good-looking man. A manly man like those who ride horseback. A man like that close to my face that should be limpid, radiating morning, a face full of that morning, a man like that close to my sticky crevices, close to my naked languid body.

"Is this Pernambuco territory?" I asked.

"Yes, it's Pernambuco."

"And that buzzing noise?"

"On the other side of that hill a war is starting."

"A war? But what war?" I sat up, surprised and disbelieving.

"A war that'll head southward on the BR that take cars to São Paulo and brings cars from São Paulo."

"But what war? I don't believe what you're saying." How could I not know about this war? It was the BR I came on, thinking . . . that BR, I don't know anything about it . . . I got up to gather up my clothes.

"Take a bath first," the man hurriedly got up, too.

"Have a bath and calm down," he repeated. "There's a watershed runs just behind here. Come on. I'll tell you what's going on. You've been traveling in the backlands for a long time, you couldn't have known about it. Where are you heading for?"

"Tijucopapo," I said, hesitantly following the man outside.

"Tijucopapo . . . that's the best place; you're going to the exact spot the uprising took place. The women of Tijucopapo are the first armed women's group we've been able to get together . . . I'll tell you about it . . ."

The man and I bathed in the waterhole, the rain drizzling onto our faces, the rain raining on us, the rain irrainiating us, and the man and I returned to the stable, naked, me shivering slightly, and listening incredulously to the news of a war. So when I came to my senses it was raining in torrents and I was situated in the reality of a war. Things were happening in an interval of fantasies. Later on I had trouble believing it. I was shivering slightly. The man and I were getting dressed. The man spoke with the resigned calm of those who plan a war for a just cause:

"So, this is a war of conquest . . .," he was saying.

"But, will they invade the fields right down to the south. Will they trample on the flower beds?" I asked not knowing what I should ask first.

"No, as I was telling you, we'll march as a body on the black asphalt of the BR that goes to São Paulo. We'll block the road. All

98

the troops for the blockade will meet in Tijucopapo the day after tomorrow to go down in a group . . ."

The man continued. The man and I ate bread. The man and I said good-bye to each other at the stable door. The man gave me a mare as a present.

"Watch how you go. Don't go near the highway. I don't think it's worthwhile going into Recife. Recife is in flames. But if you do, stay off the road. There are military cops watching everywhere. I guess we shouldn't lose touch with each other, or what do you think?"

I was sustaining a dialogue with the man. It had been such a long time. I looked at him as if he were only a mouth moving, chatting with me. Since leaving São Paulo I had only talked to myself. The man's mouth moved:

"What do you think?"

"I agree . . . only . . . I have to get to Tijucopapo . . ."

"Keep on through the forest. You'll get there at nightfall. We can meet there the day after tomorrow, what do you reckon?"

"I guess it's all right. But this war, what's it about? What's being conquered?"

"Guaranás in the middle of the counter, lost loves, the power of the rain, of the sand and of pitombas . . ." The man smiled and kissed me on the lips. "Why are you going to Tijucopapo?"

"Because that's where my mother was born." And I set off at a gallop.

I rode like a galloping mare.

"I won't lose touch with you, Risia . . ." The man waved me on.

I galloped on without looking back. I don't know if I believed it. I don't know if I believed that things happened in an interval of fantasies. Was I still suffering from sunstroke? But the air smelled of gunpowder and I could hear bombs whistling. Everything really was happening in an interval of thoughts and dreams. I had always said that I would be a war volunteer until something killed off in me that force of mine for anything at all that wasn't just being a married woman in a little white house. But from that to a war . . . From that to a war one had to dream and to think.

A war?

And would I be able to take it?

And who had planned this war that I invented?

Who made this war into a war? That man? The women in Tijucopapo?

I don't know if I believed it.

By now I'd got completely lost. My starting point was already way back there behind a whole range of mountain ranges. And I was riding on with the desire to know the place where my mother had been born, Tijucopapo: to know whether I was really made of dirt. I had left home for a number of reasons, but to go from that to a war?

A war?

Who had stolen my plan? Was it the sun?

31

The smell of bombs and weapons exploding in the air. So there I was, then, in the middle of a war. I was galloping like a mare gallops. I rode on scared to death, exposed to all sorts of danger. Why hadn't I stayed by the side of the man? Because I hadn't believed him. I didn't believe in anything any more. If there really was a war, I had to see it with my own eyes. So could I be in the middle of a war? Was the rest of the country? Was São Paulo? Recife itself? Now I could hear the explosions of grenades, and gunshots, perfectly clearly. I was heading in the direction of the road. I felt light because yesterday I had loved a man among the long grass where mares lie down. "Are the opposite of holy sisters prostitutes?" I asked myself with no idea what I was asking. All I know is that there comes a point at which opposites meet. Opposites meet at a certain point which leaves them the same as each other. That's where I disbelieve and stop believing in anything. I don't believe in anything any more. From the moment that Ilsa is a maid in a rich people's house and I travel in Varig's airplanes that beat their wings in the paradise that is the heaven where God lives according to mama, I don't believe any more. And how should one be, anyway? Anyone who ever walked in São Paulo down the supermodern Paulista Avenue, superrich, where the building lots are all ready, constructed against you, against your stature of man versus mountain, building lots invading the space like a heavy-laden guava tree, like exposed gums, like living flesh, an open mouth, knows how. Anyone who ever walked down the Paulista Avenue knows how. But what war is this? Who's conquering what? Could the Paulista Avenue be the target? Is this a war of conquest? I began to remember all those films and books on wars that had already been put on the record. I began to notice that the further on I went, the more sparse and worn the countryside was looking. Thousands of trees uprooted and whole fields burned down. I was in the middle of a war. Would I have to fight? Would they give me weapons? Would I have to kill? It was at that moment that I caught sight of the road and two military cops crossed their machine guns in my face.

For an instant I recalled the image of the face of the man with whom I had slept. What was his name again? And what did he say about the *macacos?* Ah yes, he said there were mili cops guarding everywhere. And his name? Yes, I remember, I asked him:

"And you, what's your name?"

"You can call me Lampião."

The man said I could call him *Lampião*. And that there were lurking mili cops encircling the road like a cage.

But, *macacos*, military cops? Were these men really cops?

Macacos, monkeys, were what I invented in the stories I told my brothers and sisters. War-loving *macacos* who lived in constant battle with the snakes in the jungle. My monkeys weren't bandits. My stories were stories of battles for a just cause. My monkeys were playful and fantastic.

But now, who was this pointing machine guns at my forehead? *Macacos*, according to the man.

So, mama, my lies aren't just a dream? My fantasies – will they come true one day, then? It's as if everything were taking place in an interval of fantasies and dreams.

Monkeys.

The man was called Lampião.

The monkeys eyed me up and down. The monkeys ordered me to dismount. I eyed the monkeys up and down. I said I wouldn't dismount.

"Get down!" they ordered with an abrupt gesture of their gun-barrels.

"I won't get down!" I said, clutching the mare's reins.

The monkeys looked at each other like monkeys look at each other.

"Where are you going?" they gestured with their guns.

"Tijucopapo."

"Passage to Tijucopapo is prohibited. Didn't you know there's a war on?"

"I found out today."

"Are you traveling on your own? Where do you come from with that accent? Are you of age? Show us your I.D."

I gave them my I.D. So these were the military cops the man

had warned me about. If they didn't let me through, I'd go on some way or another.

"Get down, miss." They turned their guns back on me.

"I have to go . . ."

"Get down."

I held on tight to the mare. I'd get through, even if I had to make that mare take off like she'd never done before. I wasn't afraid of the monkeys. I hated them. I wanted to tell them I wasn't a miss any longer; that only yesterday I had slept with a certain man . . . That of course I wasn't a minor. That only yesterday I . . . only yesterday I slept with a man called Lampião. I felt like telling them:

"Come on, let me through, monkeys. Monkeys. Rats. I've slept with men, okay? I'm of age, monkeys. Of age and with my own identity. I already opened my legs. Do you want me to open my legs? Monkeys. What is sex about? Let me through, or I'll call Lampião."

Lampa, Lampa, Lampa.

Lampa, Lampião.

I dashed past them, and almost ran them over as I spurred on the mare, accelerating her, not thinking of anything, or rather thinking about whether they would kill me with a burst of machine-gun fire in the ribs. What if they killed me? How many yards had I galloped to the hum of bullets? How many yards had I galloped when what I heard was a burst of gun fire and the whinny of my mare dragging me down toward what must have been the abyss I drop into when I stumble?

The monkeys hit their mark in the side of my mare who whinnied aloud as she was wounded, reared high as only an animal can, and fell heavily, dead. First throwing me off a long way, on the way to the abyss into which I drop when I stumble.

32

Falls always have the same indignity. The road to the abyss always seems like it was the first time. The road to the abyss that follows a fall: I remember it as if it were the first time.

I was a little girl and in the morning, that particular morning, I felt a foreboding. I don't know if it was me or if it came from the day. A day of sorrow and regret. I became dejected and melancholy trying to find something to play with. I sometimes felt like that – completely lost as I looked for something to play with. Those were my days of deprivation. My old ways with my toys were no use, I looked at them with disgust, old toys that had fallen to pieces, full of holes, a rag doll that made me feel sad, it was so tattered, I would almost cry when I looked at it, unable to touch it but wanting to touch it, unable to abandon it but wanting to abandon it for something new, something I was looking for, lost in the midst of the enormous yard. I wanted to play straightaway. I wanted to have a toy immediately: my greatest impatience was that one event could only happen after another. I would have to wait to find the plaything before I could play. What was it that was muddling me up? Something or other was getting me in a muddle. Some mystery, something sinister was making me pensive and stupid. I wandered round and round the yard, round and round, a stupid cockroach. I had a horrible taste in my mouth. A taste of that mournful morning. What was confusing me? Why had I woken up that way? Only if I'd dreamed of bogeymen in the night. That was it, I'd dreamed about a bogeyman kidnapping me in the night, a night of thunderous rain, of lightning flashes in the middle of the dark forest, a bogeyman kidnapping me on a sorrel horse through some sort of chasm that I didn't recognize. I wandered round and round and round the yard. I wanted some money to buy chewing gum. But would papa give me any? I thought of buying a dozen pieces of tutti-frutti gum to chew and chew and chew and make a wad and blow bubbles and chew and blow bubbles and chew and blow bubbles so I would forget I didn't have any toys that morning, so I could chew on a sweet taste and dissolve the bitter taste which I'd woken up with in my mouth. Papa. I wanted him to appear at the window right then. So I could stick my tongue out at him and send him off to hell.

"Go to hell, papa."

I was unhappy. At certain times I could clearly tell I was unhappy. Nothing was any use. I wanted it to be winter with thundering rain so I could smash gobs of mud against the walls in a rage against mama, or so my dreams would be about papa drowning in the stormy waters of the Capibaribe in flood. I was unhappy. I wanted a toy that was a war toy, a battle with all the kids on the street. My greatest impatience was that one event could only happen after another. It was the seventh of September and I had to wait for the evening to come with the time of the parade in which I would go out in my gala dress, a day of glory. Was it being the day of the parade that muddled me up? I was unhappy, I wandered round and round the yard. At night my sleep had been broken up into fragments. Childhood is anxieties.

When I went into the kitchen to have breakfast, I quarreled with my sister. We quarreled with each other. She slapped me a couple of times, I slapped her a couple of times. She called me Popeye's Skinnyshanks. I called her a slug. Mama sent me off to sit down saying that I was to blame. I sat down choking with anger. I had always thought my brothers and sisters were vandals. I promised myself I'd get my own back on my sister later on. I became even more melancholy and bitter. I began to have a foreboding. In that instant, in the very instant I had the foreboding, a big black bird strayed from the plains came flying low in through the kitchen window, circled with its wings beating around the table where the five of us and mama were eating and flew out again by the same window uttering a cry that sounded like a cry of pain. Everything happened all of a sudden, in an instant. It lasted less than a second. One moment we had halted our forks on our plates or at our mouths to accompany the circling beast and then we woke up again to find mama standing up panting from her chair with a cloth in her hands:

"Get out, out! That beast brings bad luck."

So, it was a day of ill omen. Omens, dreams and premonitions and forebodings and presages are my reality. They always were. I wheeled round and round the yard. For an hour I played all alone at twirling around until I saw everything in a whirl and had to sit down so as not to fall down. It was one of those days when childhood weighed so heavily on me that I was on the point of vomiting it up. A day of great depth in my mind. Of diving down. Of sensations from under my skin. Of a taste like the composition of my breath. Of lights from the pupils of my eyes and of sounds coming from the labyrinths of my ears. There were days in which I woke up as awake as electricity. An electric charge, a short circuit, high voltage. Something that seemed impossible for life to bear – an electric charge paralyzes, shocks you, is closer to death than to life. There were days like that when I felt myself to be closer to death. I couldn't play. My toys would burst into flames, electrocuted. I had a desire to send papa and mama to the deepest point in hell. It was the seventh of September, I would join the parade in my shiny gala dress, this time I'd go off into battle under the command of the drum majorette, I was a discharge of anxieties. I had to be alone, I had to whirl, I had to whirl and whirl until I fell down, like a spinning top. At night I had slept a sleep of scourges. I had been stolen by a bogeyman. He had come and captured me in my bed and carried me off in his white sack into the depths of a night of torrential rains, lightning flashes, and thunderclaps crisscrossing the skies, and him galloping fast on a black horse through the dense forest. He lived in a castle haunted by the skeletons and skulls of prehistoric mares. That's where he carried me off to. The bogeyman was going to gobble me up. I traveled inside the sack shaken by the galloping, thrashed by sheets of rain, regretting having fallen asleep uncovered, without sheets, because that's what attracts bogeymen. I had always slept half-naked, without sheets.

I twirled all around the yard. I twirled and twirled. Twirling and whirling. I was crazy. I was who knows how old and I was crazy. I was crazy. Papa hadn't given me any money to buy chewing gum and I'd take it out on my sister. I was as cruel as only a Rotten Severina could be. I got up onto a stool with a rough piece of wood in my hands, I was going to poke my sister through a gap high up in the brick wall of the bathroom. My sister was having a bath in preparation for the parade.

33

I'd got up on the stool. Behind me stretched a long slab of cement that covered the ditch full of shit where I used to dream papa would drown himself. Behind me was the plain out of which black birds flew to augur the days; where toads croaked like phantoms in the night. Behind me were bogeymen hidden in the stumpy thickets, and behind me were kidnappings in the middle of the night, and me half-naked; horses galloped carrying me off and there were nights of torrential rains. Behind me were night after night in which I trembled with the fear that mama wouldn't come home; and there were times when I wept into my pillow, and threw the sheets onto the floor in such a rage and almost cried out to the bogeymen to carry me off in their sack:

"Carry me off, bogeymen, I'm a half-naked whore."

The fact was that I was just a little girl, but I'd get even with my sister. Behind me was the long slab of cement concealing the shit my brothers and sisters shat. The ditch. Behind me that plain, the end of the world, the road to the other side of the seas that were just the Capibaribe River in flood, and over which I launched myself in ships, contemplating thousands of sorrows from the window on a rainy day. I never knew if my ships would sail. My delicate fragile ships. Would they sail? Behind me the outings in the rain with Jonas and the beatings papa gave me. Papa wrung me out with his beatings. Papa was a shit. I'd get my own back on my sister. And in the evening I'd join the parade proud of myself in my gala dress. "Go to hell with my pinworms, papa and mama, with my roundworms, with my *Giardias.*" I would march proudly to the noise of the brass band, the big drum thundering boom de boom up there in front. Boom boom, boom boom, boom boom. Go to shit, to dung, to pellets of caca. The trumpets pra pra pra tuning in the march. Me stepping firmly in place. On the shit, the dung, on the pellets of caca. The plates shining. Everything bright, sparkling. Me feeling proud of myself. And me forgetting that I hadn't kissed Miss Penha's face in the Manjopi disaster; forgetting that I needed Libânia; forgetting that papa was a shit, that mama hadn't hugged me, that Father Christmas had other women and that was why I didn't get socks with pompons on, that . . . Behind me a slab of cement I banged my head on as I slipped off the stool.

So I slipped off the stool and fell into a fall like never before. A fall like I'd never felt such great indignity in. So, I fell . . . My first fall and I was a little girl. I fell into an abyss, my head banged against the slab full of shit that was not, definitely not, mine: The shit wasn't mine. Was the shit supposed to be for me, Nema? So, I was undergoing the most serious of my falls, the most undignified – on the very day of the parade; the parade that could well have taken place on that morning when I was twirling around turned into a spook with nothing to play with; but the parade had to happen on that very evening, because heaven was never close, and because events can only happen one after the other. It's not fair. I fell into the abyss that a fainting fit brings on . . . The most undignified fall. A fall is always those monstrous indignities.

When I came to there were women around the bed I was stretched out on. I was half-naked and wet. There were ten women my mothers. Ten faces of women my mothers. I had ten mothers. None of them was any use. I was so weak and unprotected that not even ten mothers would be any use. Nor ten hugs. I was in the solitary place that is the place of a fall, in almost total demolition. No mother would ever be any use any more. And there were ten faces of women my mothers. And the women were speaking like frogs croaking in the night making me tremble with fear in the bed where every night I would try to sleep through those immense nights inhabited by bogeymen and cruel dreams and stories of warlike monkeys for my brothers and sisters. Would they give me a Guaraná? When we got sick mama used to buy us a Guaraná. Would they give me a Guaraná, mama? Nema, tomorrow would you buy me a whole Guaraná for me to take in my lunch box to school? Please. Papa never gives me money to buy chewing gum. There were ten frog faces chewing gum all around me. Chewing and blowing bubbles, chewing and blowing bubbles. I felt sick. I sat up in the bed with a sudden movement, I was going to send them away with a scream, I wanted to sleep. But I didn't have the strength to scream and I vomited. I vomited with an intensity that I rarely vomited in life; and I vomited thousands of times without mama being able to do anything about it. I vomited great coagulated gobs of blood. Was I going to die? I was held firm in the arms of my aunt who poured a bottle of black beer down my throat. I was clasped firmly in the arms of my aunt, since at least I had recognized my aunt. The others were nine frogs.

"Am I going to die, auntie?"

And I vomited again. I vomited like never before. I vomited like you wouldn't believe. Auntie had made me drink until I vomited it up and felt better. I had already drunk. I was already drunk like only the worst falls can make you drunk. I wanted a Guaraná. I demanded a Guaraná. Papa, will you buy me a Guaraná? Where was papa? You were never there, papa. Papa had other women and was never there. Around my bed were the ten faces of women my mothers who were no use. Nor ten hugs, either. I was half-naked and wet, in such sorrowful abandon that only the arms of mama can console. I was in the solitary place which is the place of a fall: a remote place so remote that it's like a place that I've never been to, but where I imagine the rain goes – the place where the after-earth must be, that black earth that shelters the raindrops. I was a drop of rain, a drop of pain. The women had soaked my body and my head with cold water. I felt as painful as pain itself and I wanted to sleep. The women wouldn't let me sleep because they said I would die. The women stole my sleep from me and thought that they were soothing me with that croaking frogs' chorus. The women couldn't ever imagine how alone I already was. But was I alone? The women were disturbing my sleep like frogs, wanting to make me vomit. Frogs chewing gum and blowing bubbles. Making me sick. I wanted to go far off to the place where the raindrops go, the place where I thought I would get away from that soaking melancholy that skidded my feet off the stool and made me fall into a shit of a fall that eliminated me from the parade, the gala march, the big drums boom boom in the front. Boom boom, boom boom, boom

boom. And I cried remembering the parade that I would certainly miss. I was sure to have missed the parade. I cried like never before, I cried like you wouldn't believe. If only I could go to sleep and get away from those frog women surrounding me. I was in a far far-off place. Unfortunately, it was no use any more, mama. I cried with such a rage at the amphibious faces of ten mothers. I told myself that from then on I would always lie. That when those women asked me something, I would lie. That one day I would get away to some place or other where I wouldn't have to lie when someone asked me:

"Are you going?"

And I would reply with a lie that I had already gone. A place where I could fall without loading up my feet with the weight of mud – mud that was their business and which they had decided to make mine. They put onto my account everything that didn't fit onto their account. A place where I wouldn't have to lie to them in reply to the question:

"So did you kill Analice, then?"

When they had asked me if I'd killed Analice I said yes, as a result of them depositing on me their incapacity for killing. Around my bed were ten women's faces croaking, tearing at me, wanting to hear lies. Asking me if I'd gone to the movies yesterday. And me saying that I'd gone although I hadn't gone, for no rhyme or reason, just for sheer pleasure. And making myself believe that I was capable of killing Analice, since they showed themselves to be so incapable, crying a shitty face at me, midday, time for my school, forcing me into braids of brilliantine that would melt into their tears under the sun of that walk to school, me dead of thirst, with absolutely no will, not knowing if I was going to school or if I would make anything out of life. Me lying barefaced like that, me creating my dreams to satisfy those betrayed women, lost, given away, pregnant, adopted, not real, women of lies, whores who, like my mother, slept with my father at night after being thrashed by him in the morning. My mother was a whore. A big shit. Like Lita of the guava tree. Like auntie, the defeated drunkard.

Behind me a veil of all the thoughts, all the disgusting and bitter thoughts from that taste of blood in the mouth of the drunkard my aunt had transformed me into. It was the second time she was saving me. Behind me a veil of thoughts and remembrances poking at the rump of the mare that I had never, finally, managed to become, and then I couldn't stand it any longer and I dived into the deepest sleep.

When I woke up I was in Tijucopapo already.

"Hello, mama? Yes, I'm fine. I traveled nine months."

When I woke up I was in Tijucopapo already. I had traveled nine months. I arrived at Christmas. I wanted to telephone straightaway. But my bed was surrounded by women. There were women around the bed I was stretched out on. Good-looking, strong women, women with faces darkened from long walks under the sun. Real women? One of them touched my forehead. Real women. But women of a certain type. Was I delirious?

"No fever," said the woman who had touched my forehead.

I wasn't delirious. It was just that I had already seen those women being born, in an illustration in a book, perhaps, back in school, a book with poems on seriemas. So I'd arrived at Tijucopapo. I was there now, in that place where I could ride horses and take off uncurbed in search of the explanation which might be at the point where the beach meets the mud, the black *tijuco* clay. And then, those women around my bed had long locks made into ropes of wax, of brilliantine. I sat up abruptly in the bed:

"My fall . . . Did I have a fall?"

"Lampião's gang went to to meet you and look for you when they found your mare dead in the fields near the road . . . ," said the woman who had touched my head.

"Did they fight the mili cops?"

"Yes. You were unconscious for a while . . . How do you feel?"

"Fine . . . Am I in Tijucopapo?"

"Yes you are . . ., you're in Tijucopapo."

"And that man . . ., Lampião?"

"He wants to see you when you can receive him."

"Well, I'm ready now . . ."

The women left then. Ten of them. I could see them through the window, mounting horses bareback. So there were women like that, my heritage, women who were not my mother. They were women with heavy ropelike hair, dragging on the horses' manes. They were women I had seen born, that had to be it. They had to be it. In that book of mine, a schoolbook, a book with a red figure done in wax crayon, perhaps? A landscape? A revolutionary landscape with women warriors. They were women who were not my mother. Those women, who were not my mother, bore the mark of women who ran wild into the world astride their horses, amazons, defending themselves no one quite knows from what; all that we know is, from love. The only thing we know is that love made them suffer. The only thing we know is that love made them betrayed. Women in the defense of the just cause.

And so I was in Tijucopapo at last.

I was in Tijucopapo at last. A passage. A permit to fantasy, a sort of interval between thoughts, a single step. I arrived in Tijucopapo through a fall. I traveled through an entire abyss. In a time of nine months. Through sunshine and rain. But then things started happening. I could scarcely believe it. With so much impatience over one event only being able to happen after another, so tired from all that waiting, I no longer cared whether events happened or not. And when they finally were happening, I didn't believe it. I had waited so long that now I didn't believe it. I caught a firm hold on the mirror on the bed they'd laid me down on. I needed to believe. I looked through the window and the landscape of Tijucopapo spread out before me. A reddish landscape. An almost waxen landscape. It was Christmas, and only the walls weren't supposed to be painted because there was a war. They were at war. What did I want in Tijucopapo? What was I doing there? Had I repented?

Was it possible that I had repented, then?

So, had I repented?

I felt alone. I was as alone and unprotected as on the day of my first serious fall. I was really inside the solitude of a fall. From the day I had left São Paulo I couldn't talk to anyone. I had talked only to myself. My encounter with Lampião took place just at the entrance to Tijucopapo. Suddenly I felt myself creating my own solitude on that journey. I, that withdrawal of mine, that knack I have of existing (no one fits into my way of being except myself), that best-known knack of mine – that unknown road – would I be creating my own solitude? Who would be born of me?

My encounter with Lampião took place just at the entrance to Tijucopapo. But at that moment he pushed the door open slowly and entered the room. He was a man with whom I had sustained a conversation after so many months. After nine months. A virile man who seduced me on the night I wanted to be seduced, a night of a rare honeyed moon since by day the sun melted everything about me. I looked at the man like someone who looks at a man. I who had already been deserted by a man. "How could a man desert me?" I was on the point of asking: "How can a man stop loving?" I find it hard to believe. You know, if I had a telephone right now, I'd call Jonas: "Jonas? Yes, it's me. It's Risia, who used to love you. Jonas, I was dying but not dying over you. You knew that, didn't you? So, why?" But as for Jonas, now I was looking at another man. As for Jonas, it was a rainy day when Jonas decided to die for me. I left him standing in the middle of the plain and walked away in tears. Each person who deserted me would tear me to pieces forever. How long would I keep on losing people? How much longer would I feel pain? How much longer for everything?

"So, we didn't lose touch with each other," the man began, coming closer to the bed.

"No . . . and I wanted to thank you . . ."

"How do you feel?" the man began again.

"Inside some sort of solitude . . ."

"Solitude speaks louder than anything. Solitude almost doesn't exist. You, for example, are pretty as a lake under the moonlight."

"And you are a warrior who . . ."

"Listen, have you seen Tijucopapo yet?" and he stretched his arm in the direction of the window.

"I saw it . . . and . . . and so, so everything here really exists? Those women exist?"

"Those women . . . those women are what most really exist. They are our first armed female battalion. And Tijucopapo is the place of an insurrection."

"Do you know what the cops asked me? If I was traveling alone and where did I come from with that accent. What sort of accent do I have? Do you understand the way I speak?"

"You are as pretty as a lake under the moonlight . . ."

"Do you understand the way I speak? Do you know what the word *thing* is?"

"Solitude is what speaks the loudest . . . Do you want to go with us down the BR that brings cars from São Paulo and takes cars to São Paulo? Our target is the Paulista Avenue . . ."

"I'll think about it . . ."

I had come to Tijucopapo through a fall. When I made myself

again, under the care of a man I was beginning to love, when I made myself again, because it's loving again that remakes you, that continues you, when I made myself again, well, since as for Jonas, he had resolved to die for me on a rainy day when I left him standing in the middle of a field and I ran off in tears, when I made myself again, I said yes to Lampião. I said I would go. But first I had to write a letter because ever since my arrival inside my head was a telephone message that went something like this:

"Hello! Mama? Yes, I'm fine. I traveled nine months . . ."

On that day, the day I had remade myself, a day that was, so to speak, a day in Tijucopapo, a day where the dusk could be as it used to be so it would be without betrayals, without shamefulnesses nor losses like the ones in cities like São Paulo, a day on which, seated on the rocks, I would be listening to the weeping of the timbers coming from the grove by my white house on the green hill, as if Lampião were cutting wood for our son's swing – yes, and since Christmas was close and I didn't know if someone had been conceived in the grasses of the stable where the mares lie down – it was likely that someone would be born from the perfect act –; on that day I asked Lampião if he would write the letter which I would dictate to him. Because I wanted some distance separating me from the words I spoke. Lampião and I retreated to the middle of a plain where the flowers were red, finally, and Lampião would write the letter I dictated. A letter as follows:

So that's how it goes, mama. I want my life to have a finale like a cinema movie in another language, in the English language. I want me to have a happy ending.

I left home, mama, because it's really horrible to be poor. Because I'd scratch myself like an itchy dog at night, my brothers and sisters invading the room with an irritating buzz. And also, we were a family that couldn't stand each other. A family waking up in the morning that couldn't stand each other. A family with crinkly hair: you used to hate our hair, mama. I hated waking up at the same time as my brothers and sisters because they were vandals. Early in the morning they were always getting the pots ready. Always in a noisy hurry. They were a bunch of vandals. And I felt sorry seeing them like that getting the pots ready. I found it so revolting that I wanted to leave and avenge them. At the same time I don't know if I loved them. Everything was all mixed up. What is love?

Should I avenge them? And why should I avenge them?

Mama, I arrived at Tijucopapo, the place you did no honor to. I got here after the unconsciousness of a fall. I'm coming back on the BR which conveys cars to and from São Paulo but our target is the Paulista Avenue. I won't go by the house. I can't go home. Things are as you can see – I've found the war. In the event there is destruction, it's because there is a war . . .

I'll come down to do battle, on the march from these rustic regions here, on parade with great pride in a just cause, when the trumpet blows 91 times. When the trumpet blows ninety-one times, I'll come down as a warrior with the troop, I'll invade the BR that joins Tijucopapo to the Paulista Avenue in the São Paulo of the apples of paradise and I'm going to look for a certain number of lights, a certain number of the streetlamps on the Paulista Avenue to hang them from the lampposts in my street on that day when the lights did not light up in Recife, 1969, at the end of the afternoon, Nema going on to Pedra Branca and abandoning me half-naked and unprotected in the middle of the street, you shall pass. We're leaving, and the flag must stay. We'll fix the flag. We're going to search for the justice of the lights, and in the event there is destruction, it's because we came from regions like this one, rustic, with a harshness in the soul, with no docility, with no kiss and no hug, with scraps of food in the pot and worms in the belly, and with thirst, mama, from sunstroke and a gallows on the road to school, with no longer knowing one's own will – with not knowing if we were going to school or if we were making something out of life.

Mama, I was only waiting till I got here to turn the letter into English and send it.

Mama, that letter, a letter to Luciana?

I didn't repent.

"Mother, you had me but I never had you."

"Father, you left me but I never left you."

Go to the same hell as my worms, papa and mama, you who quarreled and got me involved in your quarrels and made me cry so hard. Go with my tapeworms, with my *Giardias* . . .

I didn't want to say all this to you. But I must.

It's not only your fault.

But, should I avenge you? Do I have to avenge you, papa, for going to prison for smuggling?

No, it's not for me to avenge you.

If there's any revenge, it'll be for what you did to me.

But I promise not to go by the house. Good-bye, mother. Good-bye, father. Good-bye, you.

I took on the command from the Almighty to go on the BR number whatever and see why in São Paulo the world happens in gullets, in gulps and belches. Me who's never taken peyote. Me who's never smoked any dope. I'm going to get to the highest heights because the command comes from the Almighty. Heaven, therefore, was close, mama.

If I had to kill someone, it'll be Analice, as people have expected me to for many years.

But I don't know if I'll kill anyone. I don't think I have the courage. My strength, my desire for vengeance, what I need to avenge, doesn't take me very far, doesn't take me to a photo of me over the announcement of "**Wanted: for parricide,**" just your luck, papa. Just your luck that I don't have the strength to transform myself into an outsider and kill you. At the very most I could kill Analice, just as people have believed I would for years.

I came through the green valleys of other peoples' farms until what I got to were flowers. The landscape of a journey is the winds and the sun of many days of solitude. The landscape I brought painted on the white sheet of paper turned into a revolution. I came to make the revolution which knocks down not my Guaraná on the counter, but those who are guilty of all the lovelessness I suffered and for all the poverty lived.

I came amidst those nights ahowled by packs of hungry wolves, sung by bloated frogs, by little crickets, by snakes lying in wait, in the midst of those nights of fake-bogeymen. There were palm trees and shacks. Nobody knew that I was wandering through the immensity of a forest. I had already separated myself too much, hadn't I? I was going to ask you to print some news of me in the newspapers, mama. For my friends. So they would know that they still held a great love from me even though I was never able to telephone them.

Christmas is coming close, mama, and I still don't know if someone was conceived in the mounds of hay in the stable where the mares lie down. It's likely that someone will be born from such a perfect act.

But yesterday I had a night of many dreams, among which was the one where I am actually traveling to avenge the little girl that exists inside me and whom I cannot disrespect, and who is a little girl seated on a throne, and who is a little girl who weeps over her incapacity for the omnipotence demanded by a long table of ministers. That's why I'm going. Because at the most I can follow Lampião. For a just cause.

What I made was a thought. The women of Tijucopapo were, finally, like me casting shade on the ground, at midday, under a burning sun, on the BR, on the road.

So that's it, mama. I want my life to have a finale like a big-screen movie in another language, in the English language. I want to have a happy ending.

September, 1980

Glossary

Boa Viagem beach: "good-bye beach."

the BR: the main highway between São Paulo and the Northeast of Brazil, inaugurated in the seventies.

Giardia: an intestinal flagellate protozoan.

Guaraná: a widely popular bottled soda.

Higienópolis: an upper-class, wealthy (mainly "new money") residential suburb in São Paulo with large houses and exclusive stores.

jambo: rose-apple.

kings-and-commoners: a loose approximation of the game the author calls *serviço do rei na boca do forno* – one of several group games mentioned that involve picking sides and one group "serving" the other in some way.

Lampião: Virgilino Ferreira da Silva, born in Pernambuco in 1897. Cowboy, bronco buster, artist, and musician, Lampião killed his first man at seventeen and for almost twenty years ruled the *sertão*, the Northeast backlands, as its best-known bandit leader, feared for his violence and cruelty and acts of unbelievable bravado when he took on some of the largest towns in the north. He was finally brought down by military police with a bullet to the head, along with Maria Bonita, his woman companion, and nine other members of the gang, in Sergipe in 1938.

macaco: "monkey," also the irreverent term for military police, with the same sort of connotation as "pig" in North American usage.

macaíba: a tropical palm fruit something like a guava, with a hard, pale-yellow skin, sweet yellow flesh, and large stone.

Pedra Branca: a town whose name literally means "white stone."

pitomba: a small, hard, aromatic tropical fruit with a hard beige skin, white flesh, and a single pod.

Poti: "moon" in Tupi-guarani (the narrator also calls Poti the "moon-town"). At the time of this remembrance, it was a very small dormitory hamlet where the factory workers lived.

seriema: the Tupi term for an elegant, long-legged tropical bird with dark-gray plumage and yellow beak and feet.

Wanderleia: a popular teenage female pop star of the late sixties.

Xavantes: a tribal group living in a handful of villages in Mato Grosso.

Afterword

We think back through our mothers.

VIRGINIA WOOLF

Virginia Woolf may have been right, most of the time. But *how* do we think back when we think of ourselves as a woman warrior and view our mother as pathetic, a victim? Where do we look for our memories, our courage, our heritage, when "mama was a shit"? Marilene Felinto's deviant version of strong women, of strong memories, embeds her "mothers" – the women of Tijucopapo – in the fantasy of a personal odyssey that in some ways parallels a legendary history of outlaws and outcasts in popular Brazilian literature. Brazil's Atlantic coastal plains were peopled and pillaged by *bandidos* – bandits who were both villains and heroes, particularly in the backlands of the Northeast. They are the predominant figures in the musical poems that celebrate the popular history of frontier lands wrought from violent confrontation. Contested and slippery like the mud of the floodplains, these lands are fertile sources for the strengths, the imagination, and the rebellious nature of the people.

Marilene Felinto, born in 1957 in Recife, lived out her childhood in the wild, untamed Northeast of Brazil but grew into maturity on the sidewalks of São Paulo. The family moved to the city when Marilene was twelve years old. The attractions of the provincial, almost rural environment and coastal climate of the Northeast, and the contrast with the intimidating urban sprawl of São Paulo are major protagonists in her life as in her novel. Playing on the unpaved streets and the empty spaces and the beaches of Recife, and listening to her grandmother's stories and her father's stories, and inventing and telling new stories for her brothers and sisters were replaced in the city with a sense of solitude. She filled the void of São Paulo with letters written to her grandparents, uncles, and aunts back home, desperately clinging to those links with the sights and the sounds and the smells, the flavor, of the Northeast. This was the productive solitude of an artistic sensibility: letters became poems and playing became reading. And from a Northeastern tomboy who survived each night waiting for dawn to break so she could go out and play and play and play, Marilene Felinto turned into an outstanding student at her São Paulo high school, going on to complete her education in *Letras* at the University of São Paulo.

Throughout *The Women of Tijucopapo* we detect the sense of alienation from one's homeland, expressed here not merely as an unexamined sense of *saudade*, of nostalgia and longing, but as a projection of exile whose source is also the loss of continuity – a loss that invokes a desire to know and surpass her mother's geographical as well as psychological and emotional "place." This desire for *knowing* and for *rebellion* contrasts with the author's assured handling of a narrative fragmented over space and time:

a fragmentation that reveals her ease in a postmodern world where, paradoxically, nothing is ever new yet nothing is ever certain, least of all the protagonist's own sense of self. *The Women of Tijucopapo* is written as a letter – a letter to a mother whose suffering is contained yet long lost inside the violently signified past of her literate, resentful, militant daughter. Throughout the searching solitudes of the protagonist's nine-month intellectual journey (a daughter's process of reverse gestation), Risia asks a three-part but fundamentally inseparable question: Can a perfect act of love procreate and, if so, should *only* a perfect act of love procreate and, if so, how can you justify, ratify, the existence of a child not born out of love? Unlike the "daughtering" Virginia Woolf's political voice suggests above, the narrator of *The Women of Tijucopapo*, the unloved child, tries to think back not *through* but *past* her mother, in order to reconstitute the "Tijucopapo that you did not honor, mama."

For these and many other textual reasons, it is ironical that the narrator of *The Women of Tijucopapo* closes her story with a direct address to her mother, an appeal and an explanation of why, perhaps, this fiction has taken the form it has: "I want my life to have a finale like a big-screen movie in English . . . . I want to have a happy ending." The text itself, however, is ambivalent about the prospect of a happy ending. The language of the novel is often passionate, hostile, and unforgiving. This narrative point of view is disturbing to the feminist reader who prefers stories about mother-daughter relationships that accommodate an element of trust, or at least some attempt at conscious reconciliation. But the narrator of this version of a female novel of formation, of "growing up," is unafraid of challenging fatuities, of outraging her reader and herself as she travels to and from maturity along a lone road whose markers – countless mountain ranges lost in the distance and solitary palm trees and a squalid hut or two – map the interior landscape also, of a loveless childhood and an adolescence of abandonment.

Risia, the narrator-who-was-once-a-child, seeks recourse in memories of happier moments, in the familiar structures of religion and of play. Her religious sensibility focuses on the biblical words, grandiose and sonorous, that once succored a young soul hurt, by unfair reality and by dreams of bogeymen. And, more dramatically, trauma is converted into consciousness through reliving a series of biblical "falls" that interrupt moments of attempted revenge for real and imaginary attacks, and bring about the swoons, the moments of active unconsciousness that – like a modern version of Sleeping Beauty – attract longed-for attention, from parents, from lovers, from the women of Tijucopapo. The delights of play offer a different reconstructive escape: a haven from oppression, a safe place for the imagination, the free spirit, of a little girl who otherwise lives her life in the physical and psychological shadow of her mother's bitterness and her own sense of injustice.

The Women of Tijucopapo is, then, in part the story of a series of returns, a series of dates that fix childhood in a calendar of spasmodic, traumatic, remembrances – of taste, and smell, and noise, and, often, of delicious fearfulness. The narrator's journey starts from a highly complex yet infantile innocence that is expressed through a number of unreasoned and unfulfilled desires. "Formation" continues through a series of encounters that move from girlish admirations and resentments for her childhood peers, through a precocious observation of the dark side of adultery, and into a celebration of both the delights of "big-sisterly" love and the pleasurable immersions of the heterosexual act. Ruling over all experiences are the terrors of silent Sundays, of emotional desertion by grandmother, by parents, by brothers and sisters, by Nema, by Jonas, by the world.

Yet for all its inwardness, and despite all its explicit desires to "speak in English," *The Women of Tijucopapo* is a highly Brazilian novel. The trials and the successes of the protagonist are born in a specific regional setting and historical moment. The "original" women of Tijucopapo existed in history – they are village women who in Northeast Brazil in the seventeenth century used kitchen utensils and basins of hot water to repulse an invading army of Dutch soldiers. In this text, however, they exist not as historical figures but as the incarnation of the illustrations in a school textbook – carmine-colored amazons, strong, good-looking women riding bareback over the gummy, flooded terrain of the Northeast, where the mud meets the sand. These women fight again for a just cause, the right to live a common life of dignity without interference from outside. Their fight is paralleled and intensified in this text through another example that gives history mythic proportions. The protagonist's final, ideal, lover takes on the name of the legendary Brazilian bandit, Lampião, as he emblazons the literary landscape of war with a sweetly masculine voice of reason, explaining and justifying revolutionary violence.

So *The Women of Tijucopapo* is not a shriek of despair, it is a call to combat. The time of action is an era of civil war, both heralded and realized. The significant dates mentioned and repeated in the novel are 1964, when the Brazilian military regime consolidated its power; 1968–69, when the most violent repression moved into gear against student protests and mass demonstrations and guerrilla activities; and the present, the moment of the writing, when Brazil was staggering free from almost two decades of oppressive government into a tentative political *abertura*, or opening, and testimonies of military excesses and abuse became public. Like those testimonies, the novel's sense of alienation – the root of revolution – evokes the ambiguity as well as the urgency of resistance from exile. *The Women of*

Tijucopapo only indirectly, mythically, harks back to its literary-geographical inheritance: the violence depicted in the earlier regionalisms of the Northeast of Brazil.

Yet its feel for space, for landscape, fixes *The Women of Tijucopapo* in a world very different from the urban novels of its time. And Marilene Felinto, born into a poor family of mixed racial inheritance in one of Brazil's poorest states, Pernambuco, recalls for the reader many of the most significant aspects of the fiction of black and Native American women writers in North America: Paule Marshall, Toni Morrison, Leslie Marmon Silko, Alice Walker. They, too, write as regionally "rooted" travelers, often disturbingly ambivalent about both the significance of mothering and the violences of their society. Marilene Felinto's elusive short novel fits admirably into a number of contemporary literary currents: the revival of a new type of objective regionalism that moves across social and artistic barriers, a femininity that is strong enough to recognize its anger and fight against its incertitudes, a feminism that recognizes the "essence" of psychological self-birth, and a consciousness of the social self embedded in a history of marginal – female – identity.

The Women of Tijucopapo fits less easily into the contemporary literary scene in its own country. The best-known "young" writers of Brazil are now in their fifties, their sixties, a generation older than Marilene Felinto. The mantle she inherits goes back beyond her immediate precursors, to the writers of the 1930s, to her own favorite, Graciliano Ramos, but especially, perhaps, to Raquel de Queiroz. Born, like Marilene Felinto, in Pernambuco, and perhaps best known in her own country as a "social regionalist" of the Northeast, Raquel de Queiroz is also a writer who dealt with the complexities of female "formation": the irresoluble ambivalence in molding a single life out of both convention and rebellion.

The protagonists of the Brazilian bildungsroman, the novel of formation, are often highly paradoxical, self-scrutinizing characters. Alongside the creations of Graciliano Ramos and Raquel de Queiroz, the most memorable examples of this type of ironical soft-center include the complex psychological realisms of Joaquim Machado de Assis at the turn of the century and, above all, the intricate relationships scrutinized by Clarice Lispector, an exile to Brazil's Northeast from the Ukraine, and then to the south from the north like Marilene Felinto. Clarice Lispector portrayed mysterious women, young and old, tortured by explosions of insight, of passion, and of love. According to her literary biographer, Nadia Gottlib, Clarice Lispector's protagonists often live through a process of "de-apprenticeship" from good things in order to have the strength to face up to the bad things in life.[1] Marilene Felinto's protagonist, Risia, operates almost in reverse – her journey is a de-apprenticeship from bad memories and experiences in order to prepare herself for the good things in life. Risia is strongest when talking about poverty, about weaknesses, her own and others'. This incisive examination of debility is perhaps the most original and uncompromising aspect of Marilene Felinto's novel. It sets her apart from most of her contemporaries, and it aligns her with the very best of her predecessors.

Marilene Felinto began her multifaceted professional career as an English teacher, a translator, and a writer, even before she had – reluctantly – finished her university career. *As Mulheres de Tijucopapo*, published in 1982, is the result of some five years of thinking and note-taking. Like her text, the author of this work cannot be "read" from a singular perspective. Her own professed literary inheritance is much more classical and much more universal than my recalling of her Brazilian precursors night imply.

Felinto's early reading encompassed the great "classics" of Western literature: works of adventure by Jules Verne, Daniel Defoe, Alexandre Dumas; in later years, English texts of tormented rurality exemplified in the works of Thomas Hardy and D. H. Lawrence, and of tormented intellectuality exemplified in the works and the life of Virginia Woolf. These are writerly texts in which vast yet highly individual problems are examined in exquisite, often harrowing prose strewn over and against narrow and torturous conventions.

In some fundamental sense, Tijucopapo resembles these writers' landscapes – it lies at the crossroads of an archetypical geography irradiating a sort of conflict in which woman is neither victim nor spoils of war, but a belligerent participant in the larger scheme of history.[2] Marilene Felinto, however, admires their prose but does not identify with those great, dead, European cultural monuments. Nor does she identify with any of her own country's literary elite. If she did, she would be buying into some sort of evaluative sorting, inclusion in what she perceives as a roll call of mediocrity. And indeed, even though her theme in *The Women of Tijucopapo* – encompassing a sense of childhood deprivation, sibling rivalry, exile from her homeland, the search for love – is not unique, hers is undoubtedly an extraordinary voice. On the cover of *Postcard*, her book of short stories published in 1991, Marilene Felinto's contemporary and fellow countryman, João Camilo Penna, remarks: "Hers is a solitary place in contemporary Brazilian narrative, a marker in the desert that for many years has threatened to engulf this area of our literature. She is the tree of possibilities, that emerges from who knows what effects of genius, but which is so entirely root and earth and life."[3]

While I was translating *As Mulheres*, I was able to meet Marilene Felinto and gain some insights into her intellectual strengths and literary brilliance. She is generous, and unremitting in her demands on others; she is clever, and intolerant of fools. And perhaps now – after her first lengthy visit to California – she may be slightly less enthusiastic about the Hollywood life-style that she once narrowly and benignly perceived as an art form comprising "movies in the English language" and "happy endings."

Like her view of Sunset Boulevard, the view of Marilene Felinto from North America may also have been too romantic to survive an actual encounter. Marilene Felinto has been hailed in the United States as an important new black woman writer giving voice to the experiences of the marginal in society. But Marilene Felinto herself prefers not to be categorized so specifically. She tells us: "Whenever I sit down to write . . . I don't write as a woman, or as a black woman, or as a poor woman or as a Northeast woman . . . though I know that my literature is the literature of a woman, because I am a woman . . . and I can't escape that, and I don't want to escape that. . . . [But] the best literature and the best art should be all-embracing."[4]

Perhaps we *should* ask, as Marilene Felinto urges us to do, whether the sort of "academic-speak" we still learn in the United States, a reactionary urge to "classify" and "locate" both text and author, actually does not enhance their significance but restricts it, and does a disservice to both the poeticity and the personality of literature? Nevertheless, we cannot help but recognize and celebrate the narrative voice of *The Women of Tijucopapo* as a *woman's* voice, a letter from the edge, struggling for the right to speak for itself and conquering that right through a journey toward self-discovery and partial knowledge, and love.

The authorial voice behind Risia, born of the rude oral cultures of the Northeast, is a difficult one to listen to. Unlike that of the narrator of *The Women of Tijucopapo*, it seems consciously displeasant, brooks no response, invites no dialogue.

But as we listen, we recognize in Marilene Felinto's biographical fiction a new "woman's novel of formation": one characterized by an anarchic spirit that flails at injustice and platitudes; a spirit that *wants* to wage war, with the discomfiting weapons of intelligence, complex writing, and fearless honesty.

Irene Matthews

NOTES

1. Nadia Gottlib, interview with Irene Matthews, Belo Horizonte, Brazil, July 1992.
2. I am paraphrasing an observation in Haquira Osakabe's review of *As Mulheres de Tijucopapo*, in *Folhetím*, Sáo Paulo, Oct. 24, 1982, p.3.
3. My translation of Camilo Penna's words. *Postcard* is published by Iluminuras (Sáo Paulo, 1991).
4. Marilene Felinto, interview with Irene Matthews, Sáo Paulo, June 1992.

Volumes in the Latin American
Women Writers series include:

The Youngest Doll
By Rosario Ferré

Mean Woman
By Alicia Borinsky
Translated by Cola Franzen

Industrial Park
By Patricia Galvão (Pagu)
Translated by Elizabeth
Jackson and
K. David Jackson

About this book:
Typeface: Trump medieval.
It was typeset in house,
printed by Bookcrafters and
designed by Dika Eckersley